LoveTonics

Love is it's own tonic

I am the soul in your body,

　　　You are the soul in mine......

I am the words of your speech,

   You are the speech in my voice......

I am the tears rolling off your eyes,

   You are the pain that makes me cry.......

I am the hidden love in you

   You are love in me I want to hide.....

I am lost in you,

   You find you in me.......

And people think we are two individual identities who are separable...........

ACKNOWLEDGEMENT

I am grateful to God for everything he has given to me. I am grateful for all the comforts and hardships he has showered on me in my life tenure so far. I didn't even realise that each obstacle which was coming on my way, was actually conspiring to make me strong.

I am grateful to all the people who have left me alone in the crowd. If at all you were there with me, I would have never been able to be myself.

I am grateful to all the people who stood by me in my tough times, it is due to your courtesy, I still do trust in relationships.

I am grateful to my son PRITISH for coming in my life and explaining to me, the true meaning of completeness and happiness.

The list of gratitude further continues with the names Dinesh, Ankush, Mom.

Thank you Sandeep for your editorial service, thank you Prakhyat for your designing service.

Dedicated to YOU,

Remember that I AM ME AND
THAT NO ONE CAN BE.

CHAPTER 1

'**C**heck and mate, this is the third time I am winning,' gloated Risha while she stood up on the bed and raised her hands up in the air to announce her victory.

'Today is not my day, white is not my colour,' I said with a pinch of dismay in my eyes, I laid on my stomach on the bed I lost the friendly chess match to my cousin Risha for the third time in a row.

'But Shonali di, I don't understand your morning chess work out, who plays chess early in the morning, people go out for morning walk and you irk me every day with this boring chess game early in the morning,' complained Risha while she got off the bed and dragged herself towards the small kitchen to prepare coffee for us. We shared 1 BHK apartment in the city of dreams, Mumbai.

'Do I need to workout?' I ignored Risha's complaint and jumped out of the bed, I stood in front of the full length mirror to scrutinize my zero size figure which barely needed a work out. Blessed are few people with excellent metabolism; they can eat all they want and still stay fit, I was one of those lucky lass. Not only my zero size body but also my beautiful hazelnut eyes which contrasted my fair complexion, black wavy long hair, my sleek nose which ran down to perfectly shaped lips casted a prepossessing image on the reflecting surface. My selfies clearly portray this. In fact I was so obsessed with the perfect selfie click that I suffered from selfie elbow, the excruciating pain in the elbow which occurred due to clicking thousand selfies in a day, blimey.

'Chess is my way of work out, it is an epitome of mental exercise for me,' I said when I finished monitoring my zero size body in the mirror. I was right; though I was not in a need of a physical work out, but the mental work out was a prime modicum for my current job as an assistant editor for the lifestyle magazine 'ADD IT TUDE.'

'Anyways, thank you Shonali di, it's because of this chess game, I have a series of successful dates with boys,' said Risha while she poured the coffee in two mugs which had imprints of high heels and stilettoes on it.

'Only my sister on planet earth can relate chess with dating boys,' I mocked at her when I helped myself with a mug of coffee.

'It is identical to dating boys,' said Risha, she continued while she sipped in some hot coffee from her mug, 'Their is a lot of strategy involved and sometimes you have to be a bit sneaky in positioning, you don't want to give away your game plan too early or you might get outmanoeuvred, you can bait a trap, then it's exciting to wait for your opponent to make a next move. Both boys and chess partners, like a good game; if its is too easy to win, they loose interest and if its too difficult, they still loose interest. Hence chess and dating are games of strategy,' explained Risha while I looked up at her with bewilderment, my jaws dropped. I was mutated to a state of being stupor from sanity, I couldn't believe the sermon I heard was delivered by my younger sister who was mere a zygote in my dear 'pishi maa's' uterus when I was seven years old and to add on to my bewilderment, I recalled that Risha could barely speak in toto language and hardly crawled around the home when I already attained my age of puberty.

'Not really, love isn't a game,' I said while I kept my amazement aside along with the coffee mug and grabbed my towel to head for shower.

'Ping, sorry to burst your harlequin bubble, but how many successful dates did you had in past?' Mocked Risha when Shonali was already in washroom.

I didn't had answer to her question, because my previous relationships turned out to be disastrous, leaving me heart broken and tissue paper ridden, each time.

I revived my previous relation ship with the Punjabi boy Balvinder Chaddha aka Billoo Chaddha, he was a well built male in his early thirties and a complete fitness enthusiast, his height 6 feet 2 inch, had craned my sleek neck and gave it a jerk umpteen numbers of times, but I 'loved' him and he 'loved' me, we were a 'romantic' couple. We were so 'romantic' that on one such 'romantic' dates, I swore on my tiny waist to never ever ever ever ever (I don't want to fill the pages of this sacred letter to you with the word 'ever') see Billoo again, it all happened after Billoo was five shots down and the well built hulk started crying and howling like a five years old kid over his defeat in the bullock cart race which was held last year in his village, back in Punjab. He rejected me because he thought I was unlucky for him.

A sudden gush of warm water from the shower hauled me to present from the dreadful past moment, only to drag me in near past to my yet another ex-boyfriend 'Akshay Kumar'. No, not the Bollywood actor Akshay Kumar, but his fan who christened himself as Akshay Kumar. P.S: I was also an Akshay Kumar fan and that was the only reason for me to date the duplicate 'Akshay Kumar'. We shared a beautiful relationship until one day when Akshay introduced me to his 'small family', which comprised of only 54 members, they were so well knit and close to each other that they shared a common roof in a small village in Punjab, the other reason which added up to the break up was that Akshay Kumar's real name was 'Duggu Singh Gugga' and I got goose bumps with the thought of being called as Mrs. Shonali Singh Gugga, than I realised his need to steal the name from the super star, Akshay Kumar. To add on to my dismay Duggu Singh Gugga rejected me because I was seeking commitment.

And of course, I also reverberated my third and the last ex boy friend who also happened to be a Punjabi co-incidentally, an over obsessed 'perfect guy' who was proud of being a green card holder. He was a 'perfect guy' with perfect looks, perfect home, perfect car, perfect cooking skills, perfectly arranged wardrobe, a perfect and tidy relationship which landed up me in a police station for detention because of his obsession and compulsive perfection. On a dinner date with the 'perfect guy', I happened to wear a white shirt and the perfect guy noticed that the shirt's button was off and missing. The 'perfect guy' ripped off the extra button and some how arranged a needle with the thread running behind it's eye. The guy tucked the button on my shirt and when he tried to pluck the thread with his teeth, one of the guest in the 'perfect' five star hotel was offended and ashamed, they presumed that the 'perfect guy' was sucking my boobs in public, so they called up the cops to fix the matter. Me and the 'perfect guy' were detained in police station until two in the morning. The only two ways out were; to clearly listen the big sermon of the cop and the other way was of course putting some money on the cop's cold hands, but unfortunately the 'perfect guy' only carried credit cards and no cash, which created a hole in my Gucci wallet. We finally broke up because the sophisticated guy was cheating on me with her personal assistant.

I stepped out of the wash room with terror in my eyes, my slender body was draped in towel and droplets of water dribbling from my wet hair couldn't make my appearance sexy and appealing due to horrified thoughts of my ex-boyfriends.

'Punjabi guys are strictly stroked out of my credential list,' I said to Risha while I dried my wet hair with the blow drier.

'Come on Shonali di, that so unfair, you can't blame the entire ethnicity just because you had unsuccessful relationships in past. Punjabis are so good on bed,' said Risha.

'And how do you know that?' I looked at her with a susceptible sororal look.

'umm hm, my friends told me,' Risha babbled.

I ignored Risha and dressed my self in a jeans and sky blue kurti, my wardrobe was a Venn diagram which consisted of cotton kurtis which I usually paired with leggings or denims. I streaked my hazel brown eyes with kohl and brushed my long hair to tie them up into a long perfect ponytail. I made my way towards the kitchen and whisked broken eggs vigorously with a whisker.

'Shonali di, I think Kartik Patel is an ideal guy for you, Why don't you date him? He is perfect for you,' suggested Risha.

Shonali stopped whisking as she heard Kartik's name and her heart skipped a beat. I have been friends with Kartik Patel who also played to be my boss and the editor of the lifestyle magazine 'ADD IT TUDE' also the owner of well renowned publishing house, 'EAST MEETS WEST', ever since five years when I flew down to Mumbai from Kolkata with the dream to become an independent women; which I managed to achieve but the other dream to find the guy of my dreams was still a dream. THE GUY OF MY DREAM*, came with an asterisk mark; terms and conditions apply. My terms and conditions were so lengthy that if I wrote them on toilet paper roll, the entire roll would fill up and if I strolled with it, the trail would follow me up to metres on the road. The lengthy list included that the guy should be a non Punjabi, preferably Bengali. The guy must be a professional, a doctor or an architect. A joint family was a strict 'no'. The guy should be blessed with cooking skills as good as a chef so that I could play the connoisseur at home, etcetera. The list continued.

'Initially when I came to Mumbai, I wanted to date Kartik, I had a huge crush on him, but the only problem was ......' I paused to intrigue Risha.

'What was the problem?' Risha leaned towards me excitedly, and curiously was waiting for me to continue.

'That he is a gay,' I continued.

'What????' Risha said in shock. Can you imagine the diegesis? My first crush in the city was a gay.

CHAPTER 2

I parked my car at the regular parking spot adjoining to the office edifice. I reminded myself to collect the car keys before they get locked in the car so that I save my self from the mishap which happened often. I hastily ascended the stairs to fifth floor, where the office was situated.

'Miss Sen, I want you in my cabin,' No sooner did I landed in office, than Kartik demanded to see me personally. Eighty pair of eyes followed me on the way to cabin. Practically the entire office worked on the same floor, the digital and designing team, vision team, the planning lot, finance team etcetera.

'Don't tell me that it happened again,' I in a presumptuous tone before Kartik uttered a word.

'How could you even get such stuff printed? Were your senses out for a leave?' Scolded Kartik while he pointed out to an article in the magazine, he stood in an akimbo behind his huge, elevated presidential style cherry wood desk, the wall of the window offered a breath taking view of the Mumbai city skyline which merged with the endless Arabian sea in a seamless union. No hills no tree, a tiny dot broke the monotony- a small fishing boat.

'I know that, the article 'Choose wise colours for an erotic sex' is absurd and it is a senseless material to print, but it was my last resort,' I tried to explain while I forced my self to steal my glance from the mesmerising oceanic view and focus on Kartik.

'Who has written it?' Kartik demanded to know the intelligent journo of his office behind the master piece.

'Your favourite journo, Swaminathan,' I answered timidly while reluctantly occupied the chair on other side of the table

'We can't keep him and it's your responsibility to fire him,' Kartik ordered while he placed his palms over the cherry wood table and leaned his body weight on it.

'But it is absolutely rude to fire somebody,' I said as I picked up water and gulped in some aqua.

'Do you want me to read aloud the article?' Kartik picked up the month's edition and flipped pages angrily, he folded the magazine by its spine and started reading aloud before I could reply a 'no', *'making love, after creating an ambience, with different colour around you, can lead you to different sexual experiences. One can do this by replacing curtains, bed covers, pillow covers, candles by a specific colour. Each colour has different vibration and frequencies;*

Making love while orange colour is around you will give you immense pleasure and take you to the heavens. P.S Make love during sunset when the sky turns to a shade of orange, it will also help the couple to grow spiritually.

Making love when the colour light blue surrounds you, you will be transverse to the clear blue sky which is profuse with cotton soft clouds to sprinkle and fill your life with the showers of love.' Kartik stopped reading further where series of rainbow colours were mentioned separately along with their benefits during making love.

I smothered a giggle way out of my lips, 'I know that colours and sex have nothing to do with each other, but the readers loved it,' I said while I offered some water to Kartik and gestured him to cool down.

'Do you want me to read out loud the readers feedback?' He ignored my offer to have some water and sat down on his chair, he scrolled on his laptop to read the feedback and continued to bluster again without even bothering about my disinterest in the feedback, 'Well the readers say that, *we pay our grand to read real tips and advice from experts to enhance our sex lives, if we have to consult a colourlogist we could happily do that. Why do we subscribe for your life style magazine? 'ADD IT TUDE'.*'

'But Kartik, COLOURLOGIST isn't a word, the feed back is wrong,' I said meekly in a low pitched voice.

Kartik gazed me furiously simultaneously he tried to keep his calm, he continued, 'Shonali, I am sorry but we can't keep him, we need to revise your team. We need a relationship expert or a sexpert and not a colour gem stone astrologer.'

'Sexpert is also not a word,' I said meekly.

'Out of my cabin before I change my decision and fire you instead of firing Swaminathan,' Kartik looked up at me in anger and said adamantly as he failed to supress his anger.

According to Kartik, I was in a continuous need to revise, update and upgrade my team. My so called 'hard working' and 'efficient' team included four jurnos. Swaminathan, who was always obsessed about colours, in fact he was so uncanny that he had a pre-decided weekly time table for clothes that he wore to the office. He wore red on Monday, blue on Tuesday, green on Wednesday and so on. Beside Swaminathan, my team comprised of Amrita who was a sick and tired house wife, Amrita was so perturbed from her in-laws that her solutions to each and every relationship query ended up to a sequence from Indian saas bahu soaps. My incredible team also included two more interns, on whom I doubted, that they managed to acquire the journalism degree by paying for it. One of the intern, Deepika, was supposed to write a funny essay on 'The Cow' during her interview session for cracking the second round to enter ADD IT TUDE', she initiated the essay like wise; *A cow is a successful animal, also he is quadruped, because he is a female, he can also give milk, but will do when he is got child. His motion is slow only because he is of asitudinious species. Also his other motion is much useful to tree, plants as well as making flat cakes in hands and drying in Sun...........* I intend to reject her humorous wits, but according to Kartik, Deepika possessed the skill to make any one laugh. He often called Deepika as the female version of Kapil Sharma, I however, hence after, refer to her as Bitchika. The other intern was a fatso, Pranay, who was overweight by nearly 50 pounds and he had a huge crush on me, the crush was so huge that if he accidently crashed on me, I would be left crushed under him.

Unfortunately, my team comprised of a colour astrologer, an Indian bahu, a female Kapil Sharma and a teenager who was undergoing hormonal changes and had a huge crush on me. My professional life was as screwed as my love life.

'Just one feed back and you wish to chuck him out? How will we find his replacement in such a short notice?' I kept my issues related to the team aside and raised my concern regarding Swaminathan.

'Shonali, hope you remember that we are planning to expand ADD IT TUDE by joining hands with MODE DE VIE the pre-eminent Indian life style magazine,' Kartik reminded, 'so we need real professional writers in your team,' he explained.

'I am not a human relationships manager, I am an editor, I can't conduct interviews every week, I am so bored of it,' I said .

'I'll take care of interviews this time,' said Kartik, I heaved a sigh of relief, 'you take care of Swaminathan,' my sigh was trapped again.

●●●●●

I left without saying anything, I rushed to the parking space and soon Kartik followed me, 'Miss Sen, wait for me,' he alluded from behind.

'What do you want now Kartik? you already screwed my day,' I said while I unlocked the car and quickly got in.

'I am sorry to be rude in the office, but outside office we are friends, remember the pact,' said Kartik, he showed me his Colgate ready for advertisement impeccable white teeth to cheer me up. I tried to smile at the ironic but professional pact between the duo.

'Yeah, I do remember,' I said, while Kartik got into the car and occupied a seat next to me.

'I understand that it is difficult for you to revise your team every now and then, but we need excellency in work, I hope you can bear with me,' he tried to explain and I tried to smile, 'Well if you are not in a mood to bear with me, at least you can share with me.'

'What?' I said.

'An ice cream,' finally his word 'ice cream' made me smile, 'drive us to ice cream parlour.'

'By the way Shonali do you know my secret plans behind the interview?' He asked as he occupied the seat next to me.

'Shoot. I bet you it is something absurd.'

'Well you have been single for a long time, how about me finding a suitable guy for you in an avatar of our journo.'

'No thanks.'

'Take a leave for tomorrow, I'll take care of interviews.'

'Cool, so I can treat Risha at McDonalds tomorrow,' I said as I ignited the car and took off on the road.

'Shonali, this is really important for me,' said Kartik after a brief pause.

'This interview?' I demanded to know.

'No you fool. Merger with MODE DE VIE is really important to me,' he explained. ' MODE DE VIE has covered a vast number of NRI readers across the globe. They are the best in the industry, this is a huge opportunity for us.

'Tell me more about them, what is their history?' I demanded to know.

'Heard of Kolkata Book House Publishing Agency???' he asked.

'Oh yes, they are the oldest publishing house in our country, right?' I replied as I parked outside the ice cream parlour.

'True. MODE DE VIE is a subsidiary. Mehul Khanna was founder of the company. Some twenty years ago Mehul Khanna and his wife Sunanda Khanna died in a car accident, the legal ownership of the company was passed on to the only heir; their son, but at that point of time, he was mere a ten years old child hence the administration and legal advisory was vested on Mehul Khanna's younger brother Anuvind Khanna. Not only company but Anuvind Khanna was also the legal guardian to Mehul Khanna's son until the young boy attained the age of majority. Anuvind Khanna is the face to the company, he is the managing director, though he is not the real mastermind.' Kartik tried to explain me.

'What do you mean?' I inquired.

'Mehul Khanna's son is the real mastermind behind the scene,' disclosed Kartik.

'Who is his son?' I demanded.

'No one knows about the anonymous mystery man, but he is the one who manages and operates the entire company ever since he has attained his age of majority.

'Strange,' I said.

'Don't worry, we have to impress Anuvind Khanna for now,' expressed Kartik.

When we entered the ice cream parlour the sweet and cold aroma of ice cream filled in my nostrils. Ice-cream is such a stress buster.

'Impress?' I asked Kartik.

'One single scoop tender coconut for me and a double scoop coffee walnut for the lady,' Kartik exactly knew my choice of ice-cream. He soon placed the order and turned towards me, 'Anuvind Khanna's team will soon fix a meeting with us to discuss clauses and terms of merger, we have to abide with all his terms and conditions,' explained Kartik.

'Are you sure about this Kartik?' I asked.

'Trust me they are the best, but they have their own modus operandi.'

Our ice-creams arrived soon and all I could hear, smell and see was my coffee walnut ice-cream.

•••••

CHAPTER 3

'Shona di, I'll have a chicken maharaja burger, some fries and coke,' said Risha while we occupied a centre table at a Mc Donald's outlet.

'Being a Bengali, how can you prefer chicken over fish, I am ordering fillet o fish for us, chicken is a food preferred by Punjabis, and I am not ordering it for you,' I said, my bigotry for Punjabis was increasing day by day. I made myself restlessly comfortable on the chair.

'My taste buds don't know my caste,' Risha rolled her eyes and said in a perturbed tone while she stood up to leave.

'I'll order a chicken maharaja for you,' I said in an apologetic tone, I soon realised that I was being obstinate, I held Risha's hand to make her sit.

I unzipped my big black purse to dig in and find my wallet, I grabbed my wallet and headed towards the counter to order food. I stood patiently in the queue until it dwindled and my chance arrived.

'Yes ma'am your order please,' said the waiter with his steel framed glasses rested on the bridge of his oily nose.

I ignore his friendly smile and bluster out my order in a single breath, 'One fillet o fish, one chicken maharaja, two cokes and some fried potatoes.'

'With cheese or without cheese?' Asked the waiter.

'With cheese,' I said.

The waiter obediently accepted my order and said, 'Five eighty three.'

I handed over a Two thousand bill (the pink one- All thanks to "DEMONETISATION" I feel lighter on my wallet now due to bigger notes) to the waiter while my gaze darted on Risha, I was surprised to find that a tall handsome and well built guy who was in his late twenties, he had a chiselled nose, sharp jaws and revealing eyes, he occupied a seat beside Risha, he whispered into her ears, as I watched, he held Risha's hand in his and drew a pattern with his long slender fingers. I strained my ears but couldn't eavesdrop on them. I looked up at the guy once again, he looked a self satisfying jerk but a dynamite among girls. I squinted with suspect, I noticed that the guy was probably reading the fate lines on Risha's palm, I saw Risha blushing and giggling. I tried to heed their conversation but failed, I restlessly ambled towards them but was interrupted by the waiter, 'Ma'am your order and your change.'

'Keep the change,' I muttered out without realising that I tipped the waiter with One thousand four hundred and seventeen rupees. I turned to leave, but was again interrupted by the waiter, 'Ma'am your order,' he said happily. I picked up the tray in an oblivious state, raced my pace and marched my way to Risha and the guy. The guy was getting closer to Risha as he leaned towards her.

'Risha who is he?' I scowled while I placed the tray stacked with junk food on the table.

'Oh look, my Shona di is here,' Risha yanked her hand nervously and stood up immediately to introduce me to him.

'This is Shona di, and Shona di this is, uhm,' babbled Risha and turned towards the guy, seeking his name, 'I am sorry but what is your name?' Countered Risha nervously while she simultaneously stole a gaze from me and looked up at the guy expectantly.

'Vikram, Vikram Khanna' he said with a pinch of pride in his voice.

'Risha you don't even know this guy's name and he was holding your hand?' I ignored Vikram and questioned Risha.

'Actually di, he was reading my palm and predicting my future,' explained Risha.

'Are you kidding me? don't you see he was just trying to flirt with you,' I said.

'Excuse me Shona,' Vikram interrupted, 'I am not that type of guy, in this year till now four girls have already proposed to me and I rejected them all. I wasn't flirting with your sister,' he paused looked deep in my eyes and continued to speak, 'even if I were flirting, what is so wrong in that? She is young girl, I am a young boy, it's very natural and common to get attracted towards opposite sex,' he said with an ease in his voice. I was captivated by his repose comportment, but I managed to hide it behind my frowned lines.

'Don't call me Shona,' I said relentlessly.

'Chill Shona,' said Vikram to pacify me and turned towards Risha, he continued to speak in an equanimity, 'Risha do you know that your sister is jealous of you?'

'What the hell, Why would I be jealous of her?' I said perturbed, in an oblivious indignant state, I yanked Risha behind me and stepped forward towards Vikram.

'Because you are boring, clingy, single, old fashioned and not so beautiful,' explained Vikram while he counted each trait on his fingers, 'I'll take my words back, you are beautiful but don't know to adorn and embellish your self.'

'And who the hell are you to speak all this rubbish about me? you don't even know me dude,' I scoffed when I was discombobulated by Vikram but managed to fake a layer of confident countenance.

Vikram uncontrived, picked up the fillet o fish from the tray which I kept on the table and unwrapped it, he began to speak while he grabbed a big bite of the junk, 'Vikram can read girls in five seconds, I don't need to know you to tell about you,' he snapped his fingers and uttered with all the credence.

My eyes widely opened and jaws dropped at Vikram's impertinent behaviour. Vikram's matey and unpretentious demeanour startled me, he exacerbated the balloon of my anger, which was ready to burst at any moment. I was confused whether I was annoyed because Vikram spoke rubbish about me or because he was eating my burger for which I paid double the price. 'You are not only ill mannered but also impudent, brazen, insolent, shameless creature,' I rebuked while I mimicked Vikram's paradigm of counting the traits on my fingers.

Amidst two way countered piquant conversation, Vikram was not only relishing on my burger but was also enjoying to infuriate and analyse me simultaneously. He masticated yet another bite of the burger and monitored me from top to toe to analyse me further, he said, 'I bet you that your relationships don't last more than a month, any guy will definitely fall for you, thank God for your curves, your appealing eyes are killer, your long hair is sin and your nose ring adorned sleek nose which walks down to perfectly kissable and spicy lips, I am sure they are as yums and spicy as the chipotle sauce in this burger, but look at yourself girl,' I was again confused by his words, whether I should be happy for the compliments I received by the most outspoken and strident guy I ever met, or I should be upset about my burger. Vikram continued irrespective of my ambivalent and obscured expressions, 'Look at your self, I mean, who at your age wears these dull light coloured oversized kurta and this messy braid is just a no for you.'

'You......' I pointed out my index finger at Vikram and struggled to find appropriate words to fill in the blanks but was soon interrupted and continued by Vikram.

'You...... please,' Vikram held my index finger like a wayward child and suggested, 'you please stop criticising your boy friends, we guys can't handle criticism, so you see your criticising nature is the culprit behind your frequent breakups,' with that piece of advice, Vikram finished the session of analysing, criticising and advising me, also the burger was finished.

Vikram whizzed when he finished talking about me, 'by the way fillet o fish wasn't good, I prefer chicken burger instead,' he squeezed the trash wrapper of the burger with his hand and kept it on the tray. He rolled his sling bag against his broad shoulder and left even before I could collect my senses to make a witty response, but all I could say was, 'It is not filet o fish it is fillet o fish where t is silent,' I turned towards Risha and said, 'he doesn't even knows to pronounce fillet and he was criticizing me, by the way is this kurta really that bad?'

My eye followed him till he disappeared, a membership card slipped out of his sling bag, I picked it up to read, FITTNESS LIFE GYM membership card. Name: Vikram Khanna.

VIKRAM KHANNA

Vikram Khanna was really not trying to flirt with Risha, he was just trying to find a friend in the new city, so I misunderstood him and was missed to be understood by him. Vikram flew down to Mumbai a week ago, he had been living in a suitcase ever since he turned sixteen and left his hometown Ropar, a small village in Punjab for pursuing higher studies in

London, he was a bright student and had incredible academic achievement which gave him opportunities to travel across the globe. His world wide expeditions flourished him with possible prospects to deal with girls of all types, colours, shapes and sizes. He had been dating girls, had few serious affairs and also casual flings, he had a never ending list of ex girlfriends and sex girlfriends. At the age of twenty nine, his vast and past experiences with girls made him an amateur at girls behaviour and psychology, he claimed that he could analyse any girl in less than five seconds.

Beside loving girls, Vikram was in love with books too. He flew down to Mumbai to achieve his long lost dream of starting with his own publishing house, he started with baby steps and intend to work for a publishing house before owning one, he appeared for a couple of interviews in the field ever since he landed in the city.

●●●●●

I rushed into home annoyed and dumped my self on the couch, I unzipped my big black purse to find my phone and furiously moved my long slender finger on the screen to type in a haste a text to Kartik.

Shonali: Am I boring, clingy, criticizing? Give me an honest reply.

Kartik: What made up your mind for an interrogation session with me?

Shonali: Just answer.

Kartik: To be honest, yes you are all of the above.

Shonali: Could this be a reason for my frequent break ups and unsuccessful relationships?

Kartik: May be. Calm down and tell me what's wrong?

Shonali: I met a guy at McDonald's and he said me all this.

Kartik: Are you kidding me? A stranger told you all this about you and you are over reacting?

Shonali: I am not over reacting.

Kartik: Yes you are, now shut up and listen to me, the stranger might have told you all this stupid stuff about you, but he didn't tell you that you are a gem person, you have the kindest heart, you aren't fake like other girls. If you want some one to love you Miss. Sen, first love your self.

Shonali: Thanks, you are a sweet heart.

Kartik: I know I am, by the way welcome. P.S I love that guy for his intrepid behaviour and willingness to speak the truth in front of my Bengal tigress.

After Vikram drained away all my peace, it was Kartik who acted as a radiance who coruscated my heart with motivation. Kartik was one such friend for me who served as an oasis in desert. I kept my phone aside with a grin and slept peacefully.

CHAPTER 4

I drove in to the parking space of the office edifice, but to my dismay, my accustomed parking spot was occupied by another car, I gritted my teeth and called for the guard.

'Who has parked the car at my place?' I inquired agitated.

'Madamji, a journo from your office. When I told him that this is your parking spot, he told me that ask your madamji to park elsewhere. I think he is new. I have never seen him here before,' answered the guard in a calumny.

'Who the hell is he?' I showered another question on him.

'Don't worry madamji, you park your car there,' the guard pointed out his index finger to direct me towards an empty space in the parking area.

Before I could argue any further, my phone ringer bleeped to indicate a call from my Mom, 'oh no, such a bad timing Mom,' I grumbled and accepted her call reluctantly,

'Shonaaaa,' her voice prodded from the other side of the phone, she enunciated my name in a peculiar eccentric parlance, she dragged aaaaa at the end composing it to resonate as Shonaaaa.

'Hi Maa, not today please, I am already running late for office,' I blurted out before giving her a chance to coerce me with her series of rapid firing questionnaire and comments. I was about to hang the phone while I drove to the vacant parking space and parked my gas guzzler.

'Listen to me before you hang up,' her voice raised. I glanced at my phone tugging it off my ear to check if erroneously it was a video call rather than a voice call. It had always been an unsolved tedious mystery to me, how come my mom's prognostication of my imminent act were exactly in synchronisation with each other? At times I would swivel around to check if she was present in my vicinity or had she appointed a private detective who was secretly spying on me? Practically it was her maternal telepathic love which was pure and devoid of quaestor instinct of human being. She continued to speak after beguiling me with her maternal love, 'Ofho, you are always running late, don't run so late that you run out of guys for marriage.'

'Maa, please don't bring this up again,' I implored while I switched off ignition of my car and ushered out, I stood leaning on the car holding my phone with my right hand and shielding my forehead from the blazing sun from my left one.

'Next month you will turn thirty, if you don't find a guy for you by then, I will start hunting a groom for you,' her onus towards me occurred more as an austere caveat rather than a concession, 'later, don't give me excuses like; you want a love marriage and not a boring arrange marriage, you want to get to know the boy before getting married to him, it is about your life and you don't want to make a wrong decision bla bla bla. Your cousin Niru is also opting for an arranged marriage and see, she is so happy,' her incessant tirade continued uninterrupted, thank God, my mind was already prepared for the non stop rapid firing session, I held my phone away from to my ear waiting for her to conclude, but her sermon was going no where close to a denouement, 'I am so worried about you, about your that particular strand of your hair which turned grey, has it multiplied? Did you use a black dye? What if a guy rejects you for that grey hair? Are you getting wrinkles? you are turning thirty, you should switch on to an anti wrinkle cream rather than your old fairness cream? Why aren't you answering my questions?' she chanted non stop. If at all there were a competition held solely for the category of breathless singers, I bet you, my mom possessed the ability to beat the God of breathless singing our very own Shri. Shankar Mahadevan. I was already imagining my mom accoutred in a white and red tant Bengali Saree, her sindoor (vermilion powder) impractically ran all the way from her forehead till the centre of her whirl, she held an accolade in her right hand and stood erect behind the podium of the ostentatious auditorium in order to deliver a thank you speech for receiving the honours, 'I would like to thank the person who drew out my hidden talent, if at all she were sincere about her life, I wouldn't have got a chance to practice my breathless talking (which turned out to be breathless singing) and that person is my daughter Sho...'

Honking horns of the cars which were looking for a parking spot traversed me back to reality from the imaginary ostentatious auditorium where I was about to hear my name in my mom's thank you speech.

'Are you even listening to me?' she grumbled.

'Mom I'm really getting late, I'll speak to you in the eve, take care and keep practicing your singing,' that's all I could say before hanging her call.

I disgruntled, soon swift towards the staircase instead of opting for elevator. My phone bleeped again when I reached the mid of the stair flight, I slide the screen of my cell phone to unlock and read the text received from Kartik.

'I want you in my cabin soon,' those unambiguous combination of words had become a perpetual patent from Kartik for further confab.

'Reaching office in two minutes,' I replied.

'Can't wait to give you the surprise, hurry up,' he texted again, I read the text when I entered the office and ambled directly into Kartik's cabin instead of mine. The same old pattern where pair of eight eyes followed me all the way towards his cabin recapitulated.

'Miss Sen, finally we have him,' Kartik looked excited and happy unlike the other day.

'We have whom?' I inquired, my hazelnut eyes blinked.

'Our new journo, he is excellent in his job, he is a London return and holds a degree in journalism with an A grade score card, he is so God damn handsome, his biceps are so strong, he could easily pick you up in his arms, his face, his eyes, his square shaped jaws, OMG he is too good,' said Kartik while he counted the positive traits on his fingers. He strolled around me in an oblivious state.

'Wait, wait, wait I doubt that you interviewed a model instead of a journo,' even though I had a vast degree of dubiety on Kartik's ability to hire people, I was excitedly looking forward to meet the new journo.

'He is a combo pack who comes with good looks, hilarious sense of humour, A grade degree from London in journalism, amazing writing skills, great relationship knowledge,' Kartik ingeminated the trait on his fingers and handed over a sheet of paper to me, 'read the specimen article which he wrote 'on the spot' while I was interviewing him,' Kartik snapped his fingers when he said 'on the spot'.

I occupied the chair while Kartik stopped strolling around me and stood overhead. I scanned the sheet to read, *'Ten simple ways to make some one fall in love with you,'* I mumbled my lips and read silently, *'Love is a game and if you want to win this game, follow these ten easy steps:*

• *Know exactly when to make your self available-: Decrease your supply in order to increase the demand; let's put this basic law of economics to use and reduce your availabil-*

ity to when in need rather than making your self available for your crush all the time, let your crush miss you and feel your absence. Be courteous but play faintly aloof.

• *Practice pupilometer-: Eye contact is a powerful stimulator of love and affection. When you look some one directly in the eyes, their body produces a chemical called phenethylamine that may make a person fall in love. People with enlarged pupils appear more promiscuous than otherwise and pupils enlarge in dark ambiance, this is the reason behind candle light dinner saga......*

'This is indeed impressive Kartik, it sounds promising and informative too, where can I find him? What is his name?' I finished reading and inquired Kartik curiously.

'Vikram, Vikram Khanna,' The door opened at the same point of time and a sharp familiar masculine voice intruded in the room, reached my ear tympanum. I turned around to face the door and my gaze met his.

'OMG, what the hell are you doing in my office?' I stood up and stared at Vikram in incredulity, my permanent cantankerous was back as soon as I saw Vikram.

'Our office,' rectified Vikram to inveigle me, he wore his pleasant smile, his hair were perfectly gelled like one of those models in the bill boards, Kartik was indeed right, he came with the complete package of good looks and excellent writing skills, he occupied a seat in his usual repose comportment.

'You know each other? That's great,' Kartik interrupted our conversation.

'He is the same guy, I told you about, you remember, I met him at McDonalds,' I reminded Kartik while I still continued to stare at Vikram in disbelief.

'So you are already talking about me, that's a good beginning,' smirked Vikram, his square shaped jaw accentuated his physiognomy as his lips curved up to a smile.

'You are the same guy? Man I love you more, I am already impressed by you,' said Kartik while he gave a friendly hi-five to Vikram.

Vikram stood up to hi-five him and met his gaze with mine, I was filled with the ambivalent feelings which included a spoon full of anger, half spoon of dismay, quarter spoon of happiness and a pinch of philophobia (popularly known as fear of falling in love). He collected all the ingredients in his basket and said to infuriate me, 'why are you always angry? Just because you are single.'

'Don't try to act smart,' I scoffed pointing out my index finger at him.

'I don't need to TRY to act smart, I am smart,' Vikram imitated me and crossed his fore finger over my index finder exactly like kids do while fighting.

'Grrrr, Kartik I can't handle this guy, I can't work with him, we will find some one else,' I passed Vikram and turned toward Kartik in a request which was more of a demand.

'I already signed him for a month on a temporary basis,' Kartik disclosed while he presented the offer letter.

'Oh no, Kartik, I shouldn't have left the interview thing on you,' I grabbed the offer letter and scanned his signatures.

'That's my signature, you know girls die for my autograph, and you already have it, see you are so lucky,' he said in a mocking tone, he enjoyed the Tom and Jerry feud with me.

I left Kartik's cabin with annoyance, Vikram turned towards Kartik and said, 'Kartik dude, though Shonali left my vicinity in a couple of minutes, she left an imprint on me, I admired her for being simple yet beautiful, modern yet archaic, pragmatist yet full of zeal, the emptiness in her eyes replenish me with an avidity. I couldn't stop myself from thinking about her, I better follow her,' Vikram smirked and followed me to my cabin where I trapped my self.

●●●●●

'Hey Shona,' said Vikram, he entered my cabin in his usual repose.

'What are you doing here? this is my cabin, you should understand that you can't enter my cabin without a knock,' I said perturbed while I walked towards my chair, but didn't sit out of nervousness. I could barely accept to myself that 'his presence made me nervous.'

'Why do you like me so much?' Vikram delivered a pasquinade at the expense of my anger.

'Nothing on earth could compel me to like a flirt, brazen, shameless creature like you,' my skittish body squirmed as I counted out his traits on my finger.

'Of course, you like me from the day one, scratch that, from the *second* one you saw me,' Vikram emphasizing the time parameter *second* quoting an imaginary pair of inverted commas with his hands in the air.

'What makes you think so?' I stood in an akimbo and rebuked.

'Your reluctance and desperate urge to repel from me, your body language says that you like me so much,' said Vikram while he uncovered the tumbler filled with water, picked it up and sipped in some liquid.

'So now you can read body languages too?' I countered.

'I can read anything,' he said while he shifted his gaze to the V neck line of the laurel green colour Kurta I was wearing.

I covered the V neck line of my kurta with my muslin floral

printed scarf, Vikram soon sensed my discomfort he shifted his gaze to meet mine, came closer to me and said in an octave dropped unanticipated, 'I mean, I can read your eyes, I may be a flirt, jerk, brazen, but trust me I am decent, you don't need to fear me,' his voice low pitched, deep and sensual, I could feel his heart pounding beneath his steel grey shirt which clung to his broad chest, 'chill, I am going,' he left the cabin in his swaggery walk.

●●●●●

       I didn't step out of my cabin for the entire day and the simple reason behind my lock in was; I didn't covet to see Vikram's handsome face. I dug my self working in front of my laptop, I had my lunch alone in the desolate cabin away from Vikram's radiating personality which turned on the magnetic field around him that everybody was drawn to and dazzled by him.

       When it struck six in the eve and it was logout time for the employees, I stepped out of my cabin to find Vikram's cubicle empty, I heaved a sigh of relief in his absence and stretched my body to relax. In a dropped momentum I chose to mosey up to coffee vending machine and help myself with some coffee. Holding the Styrofoam glass, I perambulate to my favourite 'chill out' place in the office which was the desolate back stair case, I sat down on the upmost flight of the staircase and relaxed myself after the tedious day by sipping in some hot liquid, (if I were assigned the task of revising the dictionary I would renew the word 'peace' with a new synonym which would be 'coffee' so according to my dictionary *COFFEE: pronounced as / ˈkɒfi/ (noun) meaning: a beverage made from roasted and ground bean like seed yield from tropical shrub which gives you PEACE on its consumption.*), but an evil eye casted witchy spirit on me, so called 'peace' was absent from my itinerary for entire day, the moment I sipped in the warm liquid, my ear strained to hear a feminine voice giggling from the lobby of the preceding floor. I was not one of those girls who eavesdrop on other's conversation but the familiar voice forced me to do so. I moved a few steps down and two distinct voices reached my ear tympanum clearly, I strained my ears further to recognize that it was none other then Deepika's voice, the next wavelength of voices were fraternize with a masculine voice, I continued to slink in the direction of the voices and when I finally reached close enough, I prowled and hid myself behind the wall, now I could clearly hear those two voices.

'Awww, you are such a sweet heart,' said Bitchika.

'You know till now four girls have proposed to me and I rejected them all,' if not the voice but the standard patent dialogue could clearly help me in figuring out the identity of the male. Behind the wall, I rolled my eyes, 'how obvious I should have guessed it earlier,' I said to my self.

'Awwww honey, I hope you won't reject the next one,' said Bitchika, she was easily falling in his unchanged subterfuge for girls.

'Well, only if the girl has beautiful kissable lips like yours,' said Vikram and leaned in closer towards Bitchika.

They were about to kiss and at the very same moment I ambled myself in front of the duo, I kept my Styrofoam coffee container aside and stood in an akimbo like one of those formidable school teacher, 'Deepika, back to your work,' I instructed her, I gave Vikram a look which said him that *stop your flirting business right away.*

'Sorry Shonali ma'am,' apologised Bitchika for the diegesis witnessed by me and she soon left.

'Ahhh, Shona you are so possessive about me, you can't bear me with anyone else whether the girl is your sister or no. I love your possessiveness,' Vikram feigned amour.

'You are the last thing on earth I'll be possessive about,' said I and left collecting my coffee along with my permanent cantankerous demeanour.

CHAPTER 5

I wrapped myself in a gown; black slinky full length diaphanous drape, held in loose folds from my right shoulder gathered at the waist with the golden girdle that accentuated my curves and bosom. My long black hair were tied to a neat bun with loose modern bangs caressing the forehead. A single line delicate diamond necklace embellished the neckline to which hanged a small diamond charm which rested between my collarbone. My hazel brown eyes sparkled and were covetous for love. Though it was difficult for me to cat walk in four and half inches high heels through which my lacquered red tip of the toe peeped, I managed to stride the entrance of the luxurious hotel with an ease. I headed towards the elevator which schlepped me to a private terrace, I entered the porch which was well lit with red colour lanterns and red candles. A table for two was set up to create the romantic ambience right in the centre of the terrace. The twinkling stars and the warm luminous moon shone brightly over the clear sky. I continued the stroll to reach the masculine human frame who stood in tuxedo facing opposite me gazing at the ocean which blended with a clear view of the skyline of the city, which in turn blended with the sky forming a triband, he peered at dusk which was bidding an adieu to the sun and simultaneously welcoming the cold moon over the silhouette of the night sky. I watched him from behind and stride closer to him, I was only a step away from him, I tabbed him gently on his broad left shoulder.

The mystery man turned around to meet his gaze with me and he said, 'Hey Shona, you are looking so beautiful.'

'Vikram ????' I said startled by his presence incredulously, 'What are you doing here? This is my date,' my voice raised in a state of shock.

'This is your dream date, right?' a weird inquiry arises from Vikram. He appears scrumptious in a black tuxedo, his masculine broad shoulders stretches to indicate pride, his square shaped jaws sculpts to bring out a notorious smirk and his dark expressive eyes enhances his countenance which was not to be surpassed by any one.

'What are you doing here?' I repeated my question, this time in a splenetic tone.

'I am here to kiss you,' said Vikram and moved a step closer to me to grab me by my waist and placed his lips closer to mine, he was just about to kiss.

'Nooooooooo,' I shouted out loud in the state of somniloquy and woke up to the tic tac sound of the alarm clock.

        Not only my office but Vikram acquired an access to my dreams too, or should I call it a nightmare?

'Shona di are you fine?' Risha said groggily, she woke up abruptly when she realised that I shrieked in my sporadic parasomnia. She rubbed her eyes and peered at me in bewilderment.

'No,' I answered her in a cationic tone, I was irascible when it was about Vikram.

'What happened Shona di, have some water, was it a nightmare?' Risha indistinctively reached for the bottle filled with aqua which was placed bedside and offered it to me.

'I can't handle him any more, he has to go,' I jumped out of my bed ignoring the water and squealed. I was still in a state of shock, I couldn't tote on myself that Vikram intrude in my sub-conscious phantasmagoria.

'Whom are you talking about?' asked Risha, she gulped in water herself when I didn't take it from her.

'Vikram,' I said, I was precipitating buckets, 'the guy who met us at McDonalds,' I continued 'he has been appointed as the journo for the column of relationship and sex advices,' I concluded and hurried to the washroom.

'Wow, that's great he is so handsome Shona di, I still can't forget his expressive eyes, his broad shoulders, his wide chest, how cool would it be to clung on his chest?' said Risha while she got out of bed and staggered to her feet swaying a little, 'Are you going for a walk? Why are you dressed in track pants?' inquired Risha when I exited from the washroom in a grey track pants and a pink tank top.

'No, I am going to the gym, I'll be back soon,' I informed her while I ran the brush on my long hair and tied them to a pony tail with a pink hair band.

'But you never go to gym and you never work out,' reminded Risha, though she was not in a mood for early morning question and answer sessions, but my anomalous behaviour intrigued her and demanded answers from me.

'I'll be back soon,' I didn't answer her questions, instead gave her a piece of information while I dig into my hand bag and drew out an envelope from it.

'What about our morning chess game?' questions continued to pop out from Risha.

'I am running out of my mind for a chess game,' I said while I put on my flip flops and left in a scurry.

'At least wear your running shoes, how will you run in flip flops?' advised Risha, but I was out before I could hear and respond.

●●●●

I ambled in 'Fitness Life Gym' and swivelled my eyes around the vast area to find Vikram. I stride to my left, the long stretch of cardio zone was occupied with array of treadmills and cross trainers where fitness enthusiast people were burning their calories simultaneously while gazing at the LCD screens embedded on the opposite wall, I scanned every individual but couldn't find Vikram. I reached to the right side of the gym where a soundproof room made up of glass was situated, I opened the door in a haste and intruded in to disturb the coterie who laid down on yoga mats and were practicing power yoga. The common trainer asked me confused, 'yes ma'am how can I help you?' I monitored each face to find the familiar physiognomy and replied dismayed, 'no thanks, I am sorry to disturb you,' I left the room and rushed towards the weight lifting zone where series of dumbbells were arranged in an ascending order of their weigh on the racks. A bench presses rested on the opposite of the full length mirrored wall. A familiar masculine frame, who stood up with his torso upright while holding a cable curl bar that was attached to a low pulley, he grabbed the cable bar at shoulder width and the palm faced up in a supinated grip which held his upper arm stationery curl the weight while his biceps came in contact to the shoulder level and slowly brought it back to the starting position, he was doing it with ease, he grabbed my attention.

Though I could only see his back, I exactly knew who he was, I went ahead and looked up at reflection casted on the mirror to confirm the identity of the male. Bingo, that was Vikram, the casting surface did justice to Vikram's looks. He appeared more handsome in his gym vests and track pants, his forearms clearly highlighted veins, his bulging biceps, broad shoulders and sweaty skin made him appear the most scrumptious thing on two legs.

Vikram shifted his gaze and looked up in mirror to find me watching him, he continued practicing curls and said, 'hey Shona, good morning, what a co-incidence, we met at McDonalds and then at office and now we are here, members of same gym, is it destiny or are you following me?'

'I need your signatures on this,' I ignored the swag in Vikram's tone and said grumpily.

'What is this?' Vikram stopped practicing curls and turned around to face me. I occupied a place behind the cable curl machine with and intention of confrontation with him, thus the machine stood between Vikram and me.

Vikram wiped the beads of sweat from his bare skin with a hand towel and playfully snatched the sheet from my hand to read it, 'RESIGNATION,' he continued after reading the prime subject of the letter, 'but I am not resigning,' said Vikram nebulous. The gym was jam-packed during early morning hours, I noticed two girls, one of them probably had a crush on Vikram, she continuously stared at Vikram and me from the corner of her avaricious eyes, the two girls tried to eavesdrop on our conversation but failed. One of them giggled and whispered a gossip in other's ear. Sure thing, Vikram was soon going to be the next hot leitmotif in the gym. I ignored the girls turned towards Vikram, 'yes, you are,' I said in a decisive and dominating tone.

'But why should I?' he demanded an explanation calmly while he wiped his sweaty body with a white hand towel.

'Because I want you to leave,' his musk was driving me crazy. Ambivalent feelings namely *hate* and *love* played the hide and seek game with me.

'If it is a request, your request is....' instead of being strained Vikram paused to intrigue me, he sipped in some protein shake from his shaker and continued deriving pleasure from mocking me, 'is rejected by me,' said Vikram as he grumbled the sheet of paper in a ball and threw it away. By now, me and Vikram had already become a subject to leitmotif in the gym. A personnel wearing a trainer's t-shirt and a trainers peak cap ambled in the weight lifting zone, he maintained his distance from us, he pretended to train one of the two girls but his attention vested on me and Vikram.

'I hate you,' I gritted while I snatched his protein shaker from him and kept it aside to seek his attention.

'I love you too Shona,' said Vikram mocking at me.

'You resigning or no?' I asked tentatively.

'Why do you want me to resign?' he countered.

'Because I can't stand your fake facetious personality,' I answered after thinking for more than ten seconds.

'No, that's not truth, you want me to resign, because you fear me?' he came closer, leaned in and said in a low intonation in my ear, I felt a sensational electric wave of shock traversing it's way from his soft breath to my ear tympanum and reached every nerve in my body. Carnal feelings of attraction and repulsion resumed their game of hide and seek with me. Vikram possessed the power to numb me, but only if I could realise.

'Why will I fear you, I don't see any Dracula teeth or horns on you, though you are not less than a demon, but I don't fear of you.'

'You fear of falling in love with me; popularly called as philophobia,' his voice was low but vehement. Some where deep inside me, I knew that Vikram was speaking the truth.

'That's hilarious Mr. Vikram Khanna,' I feigned a laughter to mock at Vikram.

'Accept it Shona,' he said looking deep into my hazel eyes. I stared at him for longer then ten seconds but soon realised that

I was in the gym for a mission, 'mission Vikram's resignation.'

I shifted my gaze away from Vikram and said, 'grrrrrr, I don't fear you and your stupid love theories, I hate you,' I scoffed and the self reflective anger stored in my body, transformed the potential energy in my muscles and then converted it into kinetic energy when the acceleration force made me impromptu kick hard on the one of the stand of standing cable curl machine like a football. But the only difference between a football and cable curl machine was that football don't hurt toes but the standing cable curl machine inflicted and hurt my toe sorely.

'Ahhhhhhh, my toe,' my toe was swollen red, while kicking I forgot that I was wearing my flip flops and not my running shoes.

'Are you fine Shona?' Vikram bent down, asked me nervously and turned back to trainer, 'get the first aid kit, quickly,' he commanded.

We were soon engirdled with crowd.

'You will be fine Shona, don't worry,' Vikram stooped down to get closer view of my toe.

'Stop calling me Shona, it all happened because of you,' I squealed in pain.

'Hey, may be I can help, I am an orthopaedist,' a swift masculine voice made it's way from the crowd. I raised my ears and scooted my gaze among the crowd to get a glimpse of the face behind the sturdy masculine voice. The crowd swept aside to make way for the guy in his mid thirties who possessed the permutation and combination of handsome physiognomy, a well built physique and professional skills of an orthopaedist which of course was the cherry on the cream. I was awestruck, the excruciating ache in my toe was transformed to a saccharine pain in my heart, I squirmed and tried to hide my concupiscence. He gently made me sit on the chair and stooped his body down, he held my feet on his lap and gently scrutinised my toe, butterflies played kabaddi in my stomach. With every tingle and the touch of him, my body twinge and the pain subsides.

Vikram looked up at the guy and recalled that his name was Subrato, not that they had been buddies in gym, but they passed friendly glances to each other while working out for abs or biceps.

'I am afraid that this may be a case of metatarsal fracture,' said Subrato while he still gazed at my toe.

'Fracture???' Vikram raised his concern, his voice filled with apprehension and guilt.

'It will be wise if we conduct an X-Ray before coming to a conclusion,' Subrato advised.

Before Vikram could reach me for helping me out to get up and get moving, Subrato already did the job, he helped me to get up, but my pain was too excruciating for me to move so he picked me up and held me in my strong arms, his broad and tough chest rubbed against my soft hair, his height was as good as 6.2 feet . He was utmost scintillation that I was drawn to.

It was the first time that Vikram noticed me blushing, he had been unlucky to witness only one expression on my face; rage. Watching me blushing came as a surprise to him. My lighter shade of blush made Vikram curious but he kept aside his disconcert considering my toe status and managed to follow Subrato and me to the parking area.

Vikram drove us in his car to the orthopaedic clinic, Subrato occupied the passenger's seat, while I laid in the rear seat with my swollen red toe, the pain was unendurable but all that bothered me was; to sit in such a position that I could get a perspicuous and unobstructed view of Subrato's handsome face casted on the rear view mirror, so I adjusted my seating position accordingly.

•••••

CHAPTER 6

'Park the car here,' directed Subrato, he pointed out an empty space for parking parallel to a colossal metal gate. A lucid marquee sign board stood erect above the gate which read as Dr. Subrato Bose. M.S (orthopaedic) M.S (surgeon) along with the complete address of the locus. I gazed out of the car window to read the curlicue letters on the marquee sign, a strange churning of butterfly erupts in my stomach when I read the name and acknowledged that the guy is a Bengali.

Vikram turned off the ignited car. He picked up his cell phone and sneaked a moment to see the hours, it was 6.25 A.M. He stepped out of the car and soon unlocked the rear door to help me slink out of the car. He didn't expect from his own self to be so auxiliary concerned about me. He carefully held my hand and helped me out. When I stepped out and couldn't support myself due to unendurable pain, he took my slender arm and rested it on his broad shoulder to support me, he looked straight into my eyes, his eyes filled with concern.

Vikram followed Subrato, while he unlocked the main gate and trudged over a stone pathway on the mid rift in the small garden at the porch, the green manicured grasses appeared welcoming and were wet with the morning dew. The overcast morning sky was pearl grey and the air was cold elegant. The garden was cloister by hedges on three sides and the fourth side adjoined the entrance to the clinic. It was a two

storeyed edifice, the above two storeys were Subrato's residence whereas, the ground floor was his commercial clinic. Entire property was his private chattel.

The waiting area of the clinic was large and spacious or
may be it appeared spacious due to early morning empty hours,
it was well lit by natural source, it was perky and elaborately
designed. The clinic didn't transpire like other tedious and
soporific clinic. Waiting chairs were arranged in a series and
sequences maintaining a comfortable aisle. The space smelled
faintly of floral disinfectant. The walls were tangerine and
lime, adorned by paraphernalia and musculoskeletal anatomy
charts. A huge teak wood reception desk stood adjacent to the
central wall of the waiting area. On the right side of the reception desk, there was X- Ray room, it had in bold letter written
out side 'X-rays are harmful for foetus, pregnant women should
not enter the room.' Opposite door was a doctor's chamber.

•••••

After Subrato conducted the metatarsal X-rays on me, he
excused us and requested us to wait, 'X-ray report will be out
in a while, I'll be back soon,' said Subrato while he stood up to
leave.

I took my eyes off Subrato as he turned around to leave, my
gaze followed him till he egress the waiting room. I was bewildered with my own behaviour, I didn't utter out a single word
ever since I saw Subrato, I was either half crazy or half deaf, my
sensory organs went numb. The only task I did uninterrupted
was; staring at Subrato without a pause.

Vikram followed Subrato to reach him, 'Can Shonali lay
down to rest somewhere? I guess she is in pain,' he uttered in a
concerned tone.

'Take her to my chamber and let her rest for some time, make
her comfortable, I'll be back soon with the report. You guys

wanna have some coffee? my home is upstairs, I can brew some coffee for you two,' Subrato appeared to be friendly.

'Oh, lucky chap, your home and office are at a same place, you cut off the travelling time,' said Vikram.

'May be, I miss driving to and fro my work place,' Subrato replied with a grin and continued, 'I am going to get coffee for me, do you need some?'

'Thank you, but I am not a coffee person, you go ahead and get some for self,' said Vikram, after the small chat he quickly rushed to the waiting area where I survived in pain, he helped me get up and quickly headed me towards Subrato's chamber. He helped me rest on the single bed which laid behind the curtain, the bed frame was equipped with three automatic sections so that head, middle or foot can be raised as required. I pressed a button and raised head to half lay, I sat in a comfortable position until Subrato ambled in with X-Ray report. The moment Subrato came in, my body squirmed out of nervousness, my heart paced faster, my eyes were glued on to him and my wits went on a temporary leave, he had this ardent effect on me.

Subrato occupied the chair behind the desk and Vikram occupied a seat facing him. Vikram continuously squirmed his hands on the glass top desk out of concern. Subrato scrutinized the X-Ray report carefully and came to the conclusion that, 'a clear case of metatarsal fracture,' he sipped in coffee and said. I was hypnotized by his lips, throat as he swallowed.

Vikram was worried for me, to his consternation it was a fracture, he threw a concerned glance at Subrato and soon shifted his gaze at me. He ridiculously discerns me grinning at Subrato for no reason. Ever since Vikram met me, he had witness me either frowning at him or exasperate with my own self. It was the first time that Vikram saw me smiling, he was captivated by my amorous grin, but at the same point of time, he was flummoxed with my anomalous behaviour. Subrato divulge the consequence of my affliction and instead of crying out loud, I was smiling at the communique. 'This girl is mad, she doesn't needs an orthopaedist but a psychiatrist,' Vikram mumbled to himself.

I continued to stare at Subrato irrespective of Vikram's nasty comment. Finally, after the long staring sequence, I uttered demure, 'You are a doctor? It's amazing, I assumed you to be a model, you have such well built physique, a chiselled nose, deep grey eyes, you are perfect to be a model,' though I regretted my words and I wish I could take them back but there was no way to retrieve, damage was already done.

Vikram looked up at me in bewilderment and finally perceived that my smile was not a consequence of my insanity, instead it was a consequence of my infatuation towards Subrato. Vikram banged his palm on his head out of disconcert then scooted his hand up to ruffle his hair, he mumbled to himself, 'I swear this girl has a bad choice, I mean which girl goes for a geek boring Bengali doctor, she definitely needs a psychiatrist,' he grinned and again looked up at me while I was still blushing and smiling. Something inside Vikram was not at ease, his easy composure was transpired to jealousy, but only if he could realise.

'Thanks,' Subrato replied in a puzzled tone, he too was bemused by my unexpected behaviour, he ignored my comment and continued, 'your toe needs a quick fix, I mean it needs a cast plaster.'

'Plaster?'

'Don't worry, you will not have to spend many days locked up at home, you can move around a lot, but go easy,' he said as he fidgets around to find something and gets up when he couldn't find the necessities, 'I am sorry it's morning hours, so my staff isn't here, I'll get the things I need to plaster, please excuse me,' he said and left the room. My gaze followed him, my neck craned to the left and trailed him until he left the room.

●●●●●

'Are you out of your mind? What are you trying to do? A girl never tries to initiate a conversation with a boy,' scoffed Vikram as soon as Subrato left the room and we two were all alone in the chamber.

'How male egoistic superior?' my amorous grin was mutated to frowns, I immediately stopped smiling and answered in a miffed tone. I realised that my sheepish behaviour had made it crystal clear to Vikram that I'm falling for this Bengali guy.

'I am not a male egoistic,' Vikram tried to assure me.

'So are you jealous?' I played his part of game.

'Definitely not jealous, it's just......' Vikram struggled to find appropriate words when he blurted out that, 'it's just that you have already done an irrevocable damage, now you are listening to me and do what I say, if you want this guy I know a set of RULES or you could say certain LOVE TONICS which actually works out,' he puts an effort to prove that jealousy didn't creep in his mind, he stood up from his chair and walked towards my bed.

'I am not listening to you,' I said adamantly.

'You will listen to me if you want this one to work, or else you can go ahead and ruin things with your own hands. I being a male, I know exactly what a male seeks,' he paused and looked away from me, I too shifted my gaze in the opposite direction. 'Trust me, even you know that I can help you out,' said Vikram to break the silence and awkwardness between us, I wanted to trust him instantly but my mind was suspicious.

'And why do you want to help me?' I asked dubiously.

'We can trade. I will not only hook you with this guy, but also, I will make him to commit to you and in return, you will not only make me permanent in the job, but also give me a promotion,' he offered his hand for a friendly hand shake to subterfuge, 'Trust me, I can do this.'

'And what if you fail?' I asked, my eyebrows raised.

'I will resign Shona,' said Vikram and the moment he uttered those words, my face shone like a bright star, I was happy at the thought of Vikram resigning, happier than the thought of Subrato committing to me, I soon raised my hand and high fived him, 'deal,' I said accepting the truce offered by him.

'So we become friends,' he said.

'No, we are enemies,' I denied being friends with him. How did he expect to be friends with me, I particularly despised everything about him, I despised that he was unfazed by anything, I despised that he carried his sardonic smile as if the world was amusing and nothing was serious, I despised that the girls found him attractive despite that he wasn't actually emotionally attached to anyone.

'Ok, let's bargain, some where in between, we can become frenemies,' he suggested.

'Is frenemies a word?' the hidden logophile in me asked.

We heard Subrato's pair of shoes walking towards the room and soon Vikram drew out his mobile phone from the pocket of his track pants, he plugged in the ear microphones, handed it over to me and said, 'Put on these micro ear phone and accept my call, I'm out, I'll call you from the phone which rested on the reception's desk, repeat all I say, don't utter a single word more than needed, be polite to him but don't show that you are interested, don't stare at him, ignore him, be mysterious,' Vikram was expeditious and breathlessly threw instructions at me as he started egressing from the chamber.

'Wait, how can I be mysterious?' I asked in a puzzled tone,

still registering in his breathless instructions in my mind while I adjusted the microphone into my ears. (I guess along with my Mom, Vikram too should win an accolade for singing breathless. I, me and myself would be the sole and soul reason behind the two breathless singing sensations.)

'Grrrr, there is a lot, you need to learn. For now, do as I say,' Vikram turned back and gritted his teeth before he briskly headed towards the door to exit the chamber before Subrato could amble in.

As soon as Vikram reached the waiting area, he walked to the desk and picked up the receiver to dial up the familiar string of digits which was his own contact number. Me, on the other side of the wall, held Vikram's phone nervously and slide the green icon to accept the call.

●●●●●

'Hey, I am sorry, you had to wait,' said Subrato while he entered the chamber. His hands were occupied with pair of rubber gloves, cast plaster band aid, a scissors and other surgical items.

Vikram heard Subrato via the microphone which hanged from the pair of ear phones and instructed me, *'Don't say anything, don't reply, ignore him, listen to #LOVETONIC 1 carefully, you never stare at him (make an eye contact while you speak to him but don't stare) until he asks you out for the first date. Instead of staring at him, observe your surroundings; the painting on the wall or the flower decoration or other ornate. He will feel self conscious if you gaze him much, restraint your self, let him try seeking your attention instead. Behave relaxed and approachable.'*

I abided with Vikram, I didn't utter a word, I pretended, as if I was listening songs in the wynk music app via the microphones stuffed into my ears.

When Subrato didn't acquire a retort from me, he started rolling the cast plaster over my toes and unfolded it up to my ankle,

'I'll have to cover your ankle too, though only your toe has a fracture but this will give extra support and some extra rest to your leg, this will help in quick recovery,' he said explicably, I secretly peered at him while he was taking care of my toe.

'Make a seductive moaning sound say, ahhhhhh it's hurting can't you go easy,' instructed Vikram over phone, *'but be strict, be the stern school teacher who is conscientious but also very sexy and every guy in class has a huge crush on her. Be the balance.'*

'Aaahhhhh, that's hurting me, can't you go easy,' I repeated Vikram's words, but not in the parlance which Vikram instructed. I didn't sound seductive instead I sounded perturbed, rude and arrogant.

Subrato looked up at me confused and said, 'I am sorry, but this should not hurt you, I am just setting the plaster,' his hands laid on the wet cast plaster which he was trying to set. Waves of thousand volts of electric shocks or was it 'love shocks' ran down my spine, I was immensely lost in him. Though it was difficult for me to pretend to be the person which I wasn't, but I was enjoying the love game. In my mind, I was already holding Subrato's hand and he was already kissing me.

Subrato was gripped and confused between my two countenance; the first one where I was staring at him and second face when I was ignoring him to the core. I was slowly succeeding in captivating Subrato. Though I wasn't an amateur in love and flirt game, but I managed to follow Vikram's instructions well.

'Ahh,' I feigned pain to break the silence between us.

'umm, I am sorry,' Subrato apologised with nervousness, probably that was the first time when a girl was avoiding him. With his appearance it was definitely a difficult task for any female to surpass him.

'It's okay, but please be careful next time, I love my toe, in fact I love every inch of me,' Vikram said over the phone, which I clearly

interpreted.

'It's okay but be careful next time, I love my toe, in fact I love every inch of me,' I repeated in front of Subrato.

'Of course, you are lovable,' Subrato said, he was stupefied at himself and his words. He didn't want to utter those words but they came out in a flow oblivious.

'Don't say thanks or don't smile,' instructed Vikram.

I abided with Vikram.

'Here it is done,' said Subrato when he finished dressing my feet, 'So we meet again after a week Miss. Shonali Sen.' He walked up to the pedestal sink which occupied a corner in the chamber and washed his hands.

'Say I'll think about it,' edified Vikram over phone.

'I'll think about it, I don't, meet up guys usually,' I repeated adding on a few extra words to Vikram's instructions, I looked up at Subrato while he walked back to help me. He held me and helped me to leave the bed and he made me sit on the chair.

'Well, you are taking me wrong, we have to meet for a follow-up,' enlightened Subrato while he occupied a seat behind the glass top desk and sat facing me, he opened a drawer and took out his writing pad, he started scribbling on the pad.

'Say Oh, follow up?? I thought you are asking me out for a coffee,' instructed Vikram over phone. He knew exactly where and how to pitch the conversation, he indirectly incepted a 'coffee date thought' in Subrato's mind.

'Oh follow up? I thought you are asking me out for a coffee, you know guys keep on asking me out for coffee,' I said confidently.

'Don't speak an extra word damn it, don't flaunt over confidence,' Vikram furiously banged his head on the other side of the wall and said to me. I meekly realised that my confidence was actu-

ally overconfidence, '*#LOVETONIC 2 talk less and what ever less you talk make sure that you talk sense, he will fall for your essence and not particularly what you talk, rest all is just conversation. He should only know your basic details by the end of first date. Make him want you more of you. BE MYSTERIOUS. Put up your point straight, your talks should be CLEAR, CONSIZE, POWERFUL AND QUICK.You can do all the talking later when he is yours, when you reach that point of time, he may love to hear from you, probably every particular detail.*'

I nervously smiled trying to interpret Subrato's mind set, he was stunned, he couldn't grasp my anomalous behaviour.

'Actually, I wanted to ask you for a coffee,' said Subrato after a long silence.

'*Say I am free only on Sunday evening in entire week,*' said Vikram over phone.

'I am free only on Sunday evening, you know work comes first the rest of the time, I spend time with my sister,' I said, I was miffing Vikram with my extra added words of flavour in the colloquia but I was helpless and highly strung at the thought of 'a coffee date with Subrato.'

'*Why are you talking about yourself, just do as I say,*' Vikram lost his patience and scoffed at me indignantly.

'Umm, I am sorry,' I meant to say a sorry to Vikram, but Subrato presumed that sorry was for him.

'No don't be sorry, its perfectly fine with me, we can meet on Sunday evening for a coffee,' Subrato also scribbled his personal number on the letter head where he prescribed calcium supplements and other pills, 'take care of your toe, and here is my number. In case you have any problem do call me, this is my personal number.'

I noticed that Subrato was amazed and scintillated. Earlier he might have met girls and dated many girls who were easily predictable, but Vikram's instructions portrayed me to be different from other girls, I was unpredictable by Subrato, I was mysterious and cryptic. Subrato couldn't analyse the obscure to my composure.

'Bye,' I stood up to leave and Subrato stood along with me, he held my hand and helped me to traverse out.

'Bye,' said Subrato when we reached the door to the chamber. Vikram was waiting outside, he looked up at me as if he was ignorant about the entire episode, he grabbed my hand to trudge me to the car.

●●●●

As soon as we left Subrato's vicinity and stood by the car, I was about to jump out of exhilaration, if at all my toe was fine, I would have danced frantically and frolicked around in excitement, 'Yipee, I have his number, I have his number, I have his number, he asked me out for a coffee.'

'Shhhh let's get out from here,' said Vikram, he was happy to see me happy.

I occupied the rear seat of the car considering my cast plaster while he adjusted his seat belt, ignited the car and we drove off.

'I have his number, he asked me out for a coffee, isn't that's great?' I squealed in excitement, my joy had no bounds.

'#LOVETONIC 3 You will not call him up, even if he has given you his personal number. Your phone number is mentioned in the X-Ray receipt, he will call you if he has to, but you will never call him first,' explained Vikram, *'and if he calls you, you will not talk to him instantly, instead you will call him back, also, make sure that you wait for a while before you call back. You will end the call first and also you will make sure that you don't stay on the call for more than five*

minutes, appear as if you are busiest person on the earth.'

'But why not? He has given me his number probably because he wants me to call him,' I tried to persuade.

'Because by not calling him, you are making him want you more,' he explained.

'Thanks,' I expressed my gratitude sarcastically and folded my arms to sit in an akimbo like a wayward child who has been denied of her favourite treat and delights.

'You are welcome,' Vikram took a sharp left, 'I know that I am a genius,' Vikram said buoyant.

'How do you know all that?' I giggled at his buoyancy and asked amazed.

'73 in 30,' Vikram answered to intrigue me.

'What????' I demanded an explanation.

'I have had 73 girlfriends and I am only 30,' he explained to me while he took a left turn.

'73, are you kidding me?' I asked amazed.

'I have played boyfriend to clingy girls, possessive girls, independent girls, dependent girls, girls who have cheated on me, girls I have cheated on etcetera. So the conclusion is, I am an expert when it comes to relationships and dating.'

'Holy crap, I am amazed,' I stared at him in bewilderment, our gaze met at the rear view mirror of his car, when he noticed me staring at him I shifted my gaze and he turned on the music to coruscate the awkward silence between us.

●●●●●

#LOVETONIC 1 never stare directly into his eyes until he asks you out for first date (nor do you stare him on the first, second or third date you can save the staring game for later), behave relaxed and approachable, instead of staring him, observe your surroundings; the painting on the wall or the flower decoration or other ornate. He will feel self conscious if you gaze him much, restraint your self, let him try seeking your attention instead.

#LOVETONIC 2 Talk less and what ever less you talk make sure that you talk sense, he will fall for your essence and not particularly what you talk, rest all is just conversation. He should only know your basic details at the end of the first date. Make him wanting for more of you. Your talks should be CLEAR, CONSIZE, POWERFUL AND QUICK. You can do all the talking later when he is yours, may be he would love to hear you then, probably every particular detail. Don't be over reserved also, try to maintain the balance.

'#LOVETONIC 3 You will not call him up, even if he has given you his personal number. He has your number and he will make an attempt to call you if he has to, but you will never call him first. When he calls you, you will avoid talking to him instantly instead you will call him back and make sure that you wait for a while before you call back. You will end the call first and also you will make sure that you don't stay on the call for more than five minutes, appear as if you are busiest person on the earth.'

CHAPTER 7

My phone bleeped while I was at home enjoying a short hiatus from office consequential to my fractured toe. I reached my phone to answer the call from Kartik and dug myself on the couch.

'Hello Miss Sen, hope you are taking good care of your toe,' said Kartik.

'Hi Kartik, I'll recover soon, how are things at office without me?' I asked, I pulled out a pillow and placed it under my plastered ankle.

'There's a great news waiting for you,' he said.

'Tell me.'

'We are meeting Anuvind Khanna tomorrow,' informed Kartik, his voice filled with excitement and zest.

'Kartik my fractured toe????

'He is in his Mumbai office for a day and he generously managed to scrap some time for us, we can't miss this one,' explained Kartik. 'Don't worry I have asked Vikram to pick you from home. I know that you and Vikram don't get along well but trust me, he is fantastic, there has been a substantial shoot up in the number of readers and number of positive feedbacks. His articles are miracle. His last article about '*be the balance between the formidable school teacher who is also very sexy*' is going viral among girls,' said Kartik enthusiastically.

'Undoubtedly, he is fantastic,' I half giggled, though I didn't read the article but I exactly knew it's impact.

'OMG, look who is saying a nice word about Vikram, what changed your mind?' interrogated Kartik.

My personal cognition faded my animosity towards Vikram, but I didn't ought to disclose any events about Subrato to Kartik, Kartik was of course my best friend but I believed it was too early to reveal secrets.

Ting tong

The door bell jingled in the background at an unerring point of time which gave me a valid reason to escape Kartik's interrogation, 'that must be Risha, I'll speak to you later, take care,' I promptly hanged the call even before Kartik could bid an adieu.

I trudged my way to the door and stood flabbergasted when I unlocked.

'Vikram. What are you doing here?' I unintentionally obstructed the entrance which gesticulated a *de trop* for Vikram.

'Thanks for calling me inside Shona,' Vikram slightly and carefully dodged me to scoot his way inside and welcomed himself, 'how is your toe now? hope it's not troubling you much.'

'Think of the devil and the devil appears,' I mocked at him shutting the door behind.

'So you were thinking of me again? I think you should think of Subrato instead of me,' Vikram slid out the sling bag off his broad shoulder and placed it on table. He looked stunning in the amber hoodie which set loose on his masculine physique, his hair were set wet gelled, his sharp shaped jaws smiled to the core of coquettish. I wondered how the hell he managed to look awesome?

'I was thinking of Subrato and your thought was forcefully incepted in me, so please don't over think,' I repeated the alliteration while I slouched on the couch, propping my cast plastered feet carefully over the centre table. The never ending Tom and Jerry scuffle between us filled my home with giggles and guffaws.

'Well let's keep our thinking aside and eat, I have bought burgers and brownie for us,' he excitedly displayed to me the packed food and placed it on the centre table beside his sling bag, 'filèt o fish for you,' a playful grin aggrandize his schematic face, we reverberated the diegesis at McDonalds, where we met for the first time.

'You are an angel in disguise, I was so hungry, thank you.' I expressed my gratitude.

'Thanks to Risha, she texted me and told me to do the need full, she will return home late tonight, she is busy with a debilitating class project work,' Vikram tread to the kitchen and fetched two plates for us.

'And she informed you about it but not me. Great!!!' I said in dismay.

'Stop being jealous, I was anyway coming here, I had to meet you,' Vikram placed the plates and cutlery on the centre table and occupied a seat on the chair beside the couch.

'Meet me?' I was intrigued.

'Yes, your training starts now,' said Vikram when placed the fillet O fish burger on a platter and offered it to me. He was a gentle man at times.

'What training?' I shrugged as I accepted the platter from Vikram.

'You already forgot? You have a date with Subrato on Sunday,'

Vikram served burger for himself.

'Oh yeah,' I recalled, 'and you have thoroughly procure the experience and the #LOVETONICS from your 73 previous girl friends,' I mocked at him while I unwrapped the burger and masticated it.

Vikram sits upright facing me and unwraps his burger while I contemplate him and heed to his rigmarole carefully, '*#LOVETONIC 4 we guys like to watch girls eat, we want our girls to be lean but we don't really like girls who disport that they are big health conscious and end up ordering salads instead of some good food on a date. Being health conscious should be a secret. So when you are out with Subrato, you will order some real thing to eat instead of salads,*' he bites the burger and masticated it, he continued, '*mmmmm make a small humming sound which indicates you are enjoying the meal with him and you are close to foodgasm,*' he demonstrated explicably.

'Is foodgasm a word?' the logophile in me asked surprised holding the plate in my left hand and burger in the right, still confused and trying to figure out an etiquette way of eating.

'No, but orgasm is a word and we men like it this way, foodgasm comes when a girl enjoys eating,' explained Vikram. I was relatively surprised moderately ridiculed and massively convinced by Vikram's theory on eating.

'Interesting,' I said acquiescent, the logophile in me wasn't pleased though.

Vikram continued with his theory on eating, 'Speck some sauce on the corner of your lips, let him beg you to wipe it off with his own hands, if he swabs it off, that means, in his mind he wants to kiss you,' he spoke after relative pauses after each appropriate word.

'And what if he doesn't effaces the sauce off?' I asked imbecile while unintentionally chipotle sauce squirts out of my burger and spread unto the corner of my lips.

'He still wants to kiss you,' Vikram answered confidently while he brushed off the smudged chipotle sauce from the corner of my lips with the tip of his finger. We both looked into each other's eyes and the concupiscent awkwardness between us grew stronger. The way Vikram looked at me with his covetous eyes made me restlessly repulsive and confused.

'Wow these are real tips, do they really work?' I was lost in him for a moment but I managed to collect myself and resumed with my burger. (P.S no guy can be more important than a burger)

'You still doubt?' Vikram moved away from me, he heaved as if he was holding his breath for long, he relaxed and drew out a brownie from the packet and heated it in the microwave oven, he squeezed some chocolate sauce over the dessert to make the concoct more tempting.

'No, I mean,' I babbled. We stared into each others eyes and our gazes locked, sort of tangled. Soon Vikram distracted him self and said, '*okay next #LOVETONIC 4 EATING: when it comes to dessert, you order only one dessert which means you share your dessert with him,*' My face drooped at the thought of sharing my dessert. (P.S. after burger it came on sacrificing my dessert, see what a guy can do to your food) Vikram smiled diffident and continued with his lessons, 'Order something chocolatey, chocolates are considered as aphrodisiac food and more over, we men really love to watch girls eating chocolate,' he placed the hot walnut brownie on the centre table. Brownie looked so tempting that I didn't wait for any further instructions, but picked up a spoon and dig out a heap full of chocolatey sin, 'mmmmmmm...' A moan escaped my mouth, licking the back of the spoon filled with brown molten chocolate.

Vikram watched me eating and threw an assertive grin, 'that's called foodgasm, you see,' he said.

'Wow, you are great at it,' I said, I didn't realise but a wave of natural blush shade accentuated my cheek bone, his so called theories were unequivocally viable, I was ravished by the way he confidently flaunt his love theories on me, '*#LOVETONIC 5 even though it is a coffee date and even if you are 'a die to and a kill for' coffee lover, you will not order coffee, instead you will order something cool to drink; like a lemonade, watermelon drink, kiwi coolers, or mint drinks, the reason behind is simple, it will keep you cool and will help you not get nervous. In case you are nervous, don't show him by biting your nails or twirling your hair, just keeps your hands occupied holding the cool drink and sip in swiftly. In case you still feel nervous, politely excuse your self to use the ladies room,' explained Vikram while I heeded him carefully.*

We ate the dessert and talked non stop on anything and everything. Vikram shared his weird experiences of past dates; his most romantic date, his disastrous date, date which he desperately wanted to escape and date which he couldn't escape. I laughed at each anecdote he revealed, the more I was talking to him, the more I was drawn towards him. I wondered what peculiar kind of magnet he held in him that I couldn't resist my self from being drawn towards him. I started liking him. Only if I could realise it.

Vikram drew out a permanent blue ink marker from his sling bag and bend down on his knees to write on my white band aid blaster. Oblivious to my interpretation, he scribbled something in French.

'What did you write on it? I hope it's not something nasty,' I leaned to comprehend the queer words, but failed and stopped trying indifferently.

'If you are so curious find it out Shona,' said he while he covered the permanent ink marker with its cap and kept it inside his sling bag, he packed for leaving.

'But I don't know French,' I sighed.

'That's your problem, not mine,' he said, I glanced at him dubiously, and the pink pillow flies at my head. I slam it back, and he grins, slides off the couch. I grab for it but miss, and he hits me again twice before letting me catch it. Vikram doubles over in laughter, and I whack him on the back. He tries to reclaim it, but I hold on and we wrestle back and forth until he lets go considering my metatarsal fracture.

No sooner did Vikram finished the battle, he slid the sling bag on his shoulder and stood up to leave, 'so we finish with our day one practice, I'll leave.'

'Tell me what's written on my cast plaster?' I stopped him by holding his hand and demanded an answer.

'sois toi meme,' he muttered out something in French which was out of my interpreting language skills.

'I of course read it, tell me the meaning,' I demanded the translation to his gracious words which he scribbled on my cast plaster.

'You asked me to tell you what's written and I told you,' he cunningly replied and prepared himself to escape.

'That's illogical,' I feigned sickness.

'That's dillogical,' he laughed.

'Dillogical is not a word,' the logophile, who lived somewhere inside me said.

'According to Shona's dictionary even foodgasm isn't a word,' he pointed smartly and headed towards the door to leave. I loved the one on one conversation between us.

The instant he was about to unlock the door to leave, Risha unlocked the main door with her duplicate set of keys and ambled inside. She appeared tired after the long day.

'Hi all,' she said wearily.

'Time for me to say a 'bye',' Vikram said to Risha.

'Wait for a while I have come just now,' said Risha. He obeyed and shut the door behind him. Risha dumped her self on the couch beside me and gasp a breath. Vikram sat along the chairs facing the couch, 'so how is the #LOVETONIC thing going on?' asked Risha.

'What the hell? You told Risha about it?' I blurter out with disdain before Vikram could respond to Risha.

'What is there to hide in it Shona?' shrugged Vikram.

'Shona di, I am your sister,' Risha said in a dismayed tone and stood up to leave.

'Wait Risha, let me handle this,' Vikram held Risha's hand and made her sit back on the couch, he turned towards me, 'Shona, love cannot be hidden and if you find a reason to hide it, then it's not at all love. If you like him, then YOU yourself have to accept it, if YOU your self cannot accept it, then how do you expect him to accept it?'

I was mollified by his witty words, I gazed at Risha and gave her an apologetic glance. Risha responded with an exculpating smile. When relations are so close and so well knit, eyes do the talking and words are needless.

'I think I should leave, so Shona tomorrow we go shopping for you,' concluded Vikram.

'I don't need shopping, I have enough clothes,' I rolled my eyes.

'Please Shona di get some real new clothes for you,' suggested Risha.

'Yes, so we go shopping tomorrow, I'll pick you up from home post lunch, and after shopping we have an important meeting to attend. Take care for now girls,' he said tentatively and left our vicinity.

'Yeah, meeting with Anuvind Khanna.'

•••••

#LOVETONIC 4 Men like to watch girls eating, they want their girls to be lean but we don't really like girls who disport that they are health conscious and end up ordering salads instead of some good food on a date. Being health conscious should be a secret. So order some real thing to eat instead of salads. Eat peacefully and enjoy the meal.

#LOVETONIC 5 Even though it is a coffee date and even if you are 'a die to and kill for coffee lover', you will not order coffee, instead you will order something cool to drink; like a lemonade, watermelon drink, kiwi coolers, or mint drinks, the reason behind is simple, it will keep you cool and will help you not get nervous. In case you are nervous, don't flaunt it to him by biting your nails or twirling your hair, just keeps your hands occupied holding the cool drink and sip in swiftly, politely excuse your self to use the ladies room.

CHAPTER 8

Vikram picked me up from home post lunch, he was driving us to a line of clothing outlets. I sat nervously at the edge of the passenger seat of his car, my body squirmed as I played with the corner of my rouge peach cotton chanderi dupatta which I paired with a coral shade of peach kurta. I dressed up myself according to the meeting to be attended after shopping. I tied up my loose bang curls to a messy bun and a wavy strand of hair prodded out of the bun which I tucked behind my ear. I smoked my eyes with kohl. Butternut squash shade of lip gloss played on my lips. I peered out of the window in a state of incertitude, I wasn't sure, What was in store for me? Was my decision to surrender to Vikram viable? Various such questions infiltrated in my mind, I was lost in my world of apprehension and anxiety.

Vikram sensed my apprehension, he drove swiftly across the street and initiated a conversation with me, 'how is your toe now?' he asked a simple question to divert my mind, he exactly knew the deal.

'Hm,' I answered in a lost tone.

'How is your toe Shona?' he repeated his question.

'Uhm, better,' I said while I looked up at him and promptly resumed to peer outside the car through window.

'I am already imagining you and your big cast plastered ankle on a date with Subrato,' he mocked at me, but I didn't respond to his mockery. He instantly realised that his attempt to amuse me went in vain, he didn't do any good to my fidgety and restless configuration, on contrary, I was more skittish now.

I despondently looked at the white band aid plaster, 'you have been on so many dates, but have you ever been on a date with a girl who arrived with a plastered ankle?' I asked dejected, my hazelnut eyes twinkled with hope to seek real hope in Vikram's answer.

My puerile question persuaded Vikram's mind to wander in past. After racking his brain for more than two minute, he said, 'I'm not as lucky as Subrato, but I have been on dates, where I was in a cast band aid,' he informed.

'Oh really, that girl must be special,' I amusingly asked out of curiosity, the view outside wasn't captivating me anymore, I turned myself to look up at Vikram.

'Not really *special*', I had a cast plaster for an entire year,' laughed Vikram at his memoir while he diminished his car speed considering a speed breaker. I sat comfortably from being seated on the edge and heeded Vikram inquisitively, he continued, 'I broke my wrist while playing soccer back in London and I didn't take off the plaster band aid for an entire year,' he dwells, his jaws smiled as he spoke. I was so captivated by his rigmarole that I almost forgot my apprehension.

'Why didn't you take it off?' I giggled.

'Coz it looked cool on me, girls kinda liked it; more over I liked it when girl paid their sympathy towards my broken wrist. I remember the way I used to flaunt while I brag my anecdote of playing soccer and breaking the wrist.'

I laughed at his flamboyancy and he followed my laughter in a synchronized tone, 'so should I too seek Subrato's sympathy?' I asked innocuous.

'No, this will not work for a girl, their is a different LOVE TONIC for girls in this case, *#LOVE TONIC 6 You don't reveal any thing about yourself which is depicting sad or has a depressing side hidden, we guys don't want to play as therapist on our first date or even on second or third (you can reveal all your secrets, when he is yours, now when he isn't yours your personal life is none of his business). You will not bring up topic like your past relations and the reason why they failed miserably. In case he brings up the topic, you just smile and say, 'things didn't work out,' and move on to next topic. You should appear like a soft summer breeze for him rather than a damaged and broken piece of mess.'*

'Wow, I'm sure you were awesome with these #LOVETONICS in your college days, You were the cool swagger dude kinds ha?' I asked.

'I were???' Vikram countered.

'I mean you are,' I rectified, 'by the way, if it weren't about Subrato, I would have never agreed on practicing your #LOVETONICS,' I confessed.

'Look at you, you are already in love with him? you have met him only once,' Vikram asked to confirm while he looked into my twinkling empty eyes for less than two seconds, he took a sharp left turn.

     I metamorphosed from being weird and nervous to tranquilised. I switched off the car A.C. and slid down the glass of the window to get some fresh air, I rested my elbow on the window, 'I don't know if I really love him, but yeah I know that I like him and I'm sure love will follow us,' I said with a pinch of doubt and an equal pinch of confidence in my determination.

'What is making you so sure that love will follow you?' inquired Vikram. For the first time ever since I met with Vikram, we were having a sagacious conversation, he listened while I spoke and vice versa.

'He fulfils almost all the criteria of my checklist,' I said, wondering weather I should have mentioned about my checklist.

'So you have a checklist?' inquired Vikram.

'Everybody has a check list, every body has their own types, own expectations from their partner-to-be,' I answered with modesty.

'What is your checklist?' he asked.

'He is a doctor, he is handsome, he is a Bengali, he is rich, he doesn't lives with his parents, he fulfils almost all criteria of my check list,' I counted out traits on my fingers.

Vikram stared at me and envisaged, 'and you feel that you can fall in love with a guy who fulfils your check list?' he asked after a big pause.

I shifted my gaze to Vikram and stared at him for longer than a minute, I silently continued staring at him wondering weather I should answer his mature question or keep the reason to myself.

After a brief thought I decided to share the reason with Vikram, 'at the end of the day, after a good education, after a successful career, we girls seek stability in our life. After a tiring day at office, we girls don't want to come back to an empty apartment, instead we want to walk in a place called as 'home'. We want spend weekends with two lovely kids, a pet dog and a loving husband. Though I don't see love in Subrato, I see that stability in him which I didn't find in the other guys I dated previously. Next month I'll turn 30 and my parents will start finding a *stability* for me. Before they do the job in their archaic reckless manner, I want to do it for my self. I don't want a boring arranged marriage. I want a life partner of my choice. I want to feel the bond growing between me and my partner before we tie a knot,' I said explicably while Vikram had already parked the car and sat still to let me finish. He patiently comprehended to each word that I said.

'Let's go and get going for shopping,' said Vikram. In that moment, I saw respect for me in his expressive eyes. In his view may be, I wasn't a perfect balance between the formidable school teacher who is also very sexy; but I was the right balanced girl who is educated, career oriented and also wants to make a home.

•••••

The fashion store was located in a close vicinity to our office, but I had never been there before. I was an epoxy to my favourite brand, *Fabindia*. It satiated my need of ethnic comfortable cotton outfits, on the other side when it came to western outfits, the maximum I experimented with was; denims, which I paired with cotton kurta. Thus my wardrobe was a blend of indo-western outfits.

Vikram walked in the store with his swagger countenance and I followed him meekly. I was thunderbolt by the trendy revealing apparel displayed on the mannequins. My heart raced faster, I wasn't sure whether I was at a right place for shopping, my trepidation combined with my intuitions and cued out loudly to me that, 'THESE OUTFITS ARE SO NOT MY TYPES.'

'Good afternoon Sir, how can I help you?' a sleek women in livery who was probably the sales girl approached Vikram, her lacquered lips carried a friendly smile.

'Hey, how are you?' replied Vikram.

'I am fine sir, how can I help you?'

'Well, we are looking for outfits for ma'am,' Vikram grinned, his magnetic personality captivated the sales girl in a fraction of second, she blushed and gave him a *awwww you are so cute* look. Vikram continued, 'get her something not too revealing and not too hiding.'

'And what do I get for you?' she asked Vikram in a salacious tone.

'For me, I can have you?' replied Vikram.

'That's naughty,' she blushed.

'I am not naughty at all, till now in this year four girls have proposed to me and I rejected them all,' said Vikram. (Whether you believe it or not but his standard dialogue always worked on girls) I was obtuse of his same old vacuous TO START line.

'Good you rejected them,' she said.

I looked up at the sales girl in bewilderment, I was amazed at girl's cynic responses to Vikram's doltish stimulus. According to me, either the girls are maniac to fall for a flamboyant guy like Vikram or they don't have a good choice, 'excuse me, we are here to buy something for me,' I interrupted the two.

'Oh yeah,' Vikram shifted his gaze to mine, he sensed my discomfort and jittery behaviour, he soon turned towards the sales girl and requested to her, 'please get her something appealing to wear, and please let her get rid of her sports bra, give her a push up bra,' he said candid and frankly, my jaws drop and I looked up at Vikram in disbelief.

The sales girl blushed and left our vicinity to get a few outfits for me.

'How do you know that I wear a sports bra?' as soon as the sales girl left us alone, I nudged Vikram and asked him in a low pitch tone so that I wasn't audible to anyone except him.

'I know it all,' he smirked in a mockery and his eyes were filled with mischief, *we guys don't like girls who dress up sporty and masculine we guys want a girl friend and not a boy friend who is actually a girl, so the more feminine a girl behaves the better it goes. #LOVETONIC 7 .'*

'And why were you flirting with that girl?' I pretend to ignore his rule despite of hearing every word lucid and I interrogated him in a strange combination of perfunctory and peremptory.

'Are you jealous Shona?' Vikram countered.

'Definitely not jealous,' I flaunted my fake confidence.

'I like jealous girls,' informed Vikram. I rolled my eyes and was about to continue the argument with Vikram but I opted to cut the argument, because the sales girl intrudes with clothes for me to try on, '#LOVETONIC 8 No matter how jealous you feel, never show it to the guy, I know its hard for you girls to not feel jealous, but you can always pretend that you are not affected. The reason behind this simple rule is, it makes you DIFFERENT from the other girls.'

The sales girl returned with a wide series of western out-fits; vibrant colours, sober colours, solid colours, shift dresses, skater dresses, midi dresses, maxi dresses etcetera. All sorts of women's outfits were included in her sieve. Vikram scrutinized each outfit personally then as he turned towards me and said, 'here comes the most important rule , #LOVETONIC 9 this rule has a name; I am me and that no one can be. This Love tonic is a super star. I subcategorize this rule as 36, 24 and 36. NO don't take me wrong I'm not talking about your vitals but I m talking about;

#LOVETONIC 9.1 THIRTY SIX PERCENT OF YOUR PERSONAL-ITY IS YOUR CLOTHES, choose what you wear wisely and make sure that what ever you choose suits you and fits you. It should neither be oversized nor undersized, it should be YOUR size. We guys don't really bother the label behind the dress, but what's important is, the way it looks on you and the way it fits you, the way your outfit defines and enhances your personality; so never fuss about brands, wear any subtle brand of your choice. I call it stupidity when a girl chooses an expensive branded dress which doesn't suits her rather than a not so expensive outfit which does justice to her body. DON'T over do your self with loads of accessories, be on the minimal side. When it come to accessorizing your outfits the less the better and if you want to convert the better to the best, then keep it feminine; every thing that *you choose for you self, make sure that its feminine.'* Vikram selected three outfits out of the herd for me to try on.

'And what about the other two rules 24 and 36?' I inquired.

'I'll let you know later, for now, you try these outfits,' said Vikram when he handed over outfits to me.

I obediently carried the first outfit and nervously entered the changing room, I shut the door and sat on the black cushioned stool which occupied the centre corner in the small cubicle, I took a deep breath, I saw my self on the casting full length mirror and motivated the girl on the mirror, 'relax Shona its just an outfit, I'm sure you gonna carry it well,' I stood up and scrutinised the floral print cold shoulder black short bodycon dress with straps at the back. I held the outfit in my hand, my eyes filled with conundrum peered at the outfit for more than five minutes, I was in dilemma whether I should give it a try? I again motivated myself, 'come on Shona which century are you living in? This outfit is totally cool, you at not the first girl to wear it,' I challenged my self and closed my eyes thoughtfully, Vikram's face flashed in the back of my mind, the thought that he might be flirting with the sales girl provoked me to an oodles of extent a sudden urge to interrupt the two from flirting blazed within me, I quickly got my body into the outfit and soon unassertively slinked out of the changing room without even checking my self in mirror.

I timorously tread toward Vikram and stood opposite facing him. Vikram turned toward me and his jaws dropped the moment he saw me, 'you look stunning,' he ogled and commented, I blushed and checked my self on the mirror attached to the wall parallel. For a moment or two, I couldn't believe that it was MY own reflection casted on the mirror, the outfit looked better than I expected. It fitted my svelte body as if it were made for me, my sleek legs appeared lissom, if at all my mom saw me in that attire, she would have excitedly offered an extra prasadam of coconut and many extra rossogullas to goddess Durga.

'But you can't wear this,' said Vikram, it wasn't that he hadn't witnessed girls in these kind of outfits before, but the fact that I was about to wear it in front of Subrato bothered him, a pinch of jealousy flourished in his eyes.

'Why? am I not looking nice? I told you, all this is not for me.' I cried oblivious to his rumination.

'No no you are very very very beautiful, a perfect blend of bold and modest on one side, whereas shy and demure on the other, but you can't wear this in front of him,' he babbled. He was mesmerised by my new look but he wasn't convinced. He noticed the shyness in my eyes and my reluctance of accepting myself in that outfit.

'But why?' I asked puzzled.

'Because...... because,' he babbled, his brain googled out for appropriate words to say, in his mind he had prime reasons which was *Subrato will go crazy if he see you in this.* 'Because your fractured ankle and cast plaster is spoiling the look, how about you try on this maxi dress this is a full length dress and this can camouflage your plaster,' he suggested while he pointed out to a maxi dress.

'Okay,' I abided by Vikram, 'I'll try the other outfit.'

I carried the full length bottle green pleated maxi dress to the unvaried changing room. The dress was a V neck, it was accentuated with a subtle black pearl belt to its waist. I quickly put it on and stepped out of the changing room with more confidence than the previous time. The belt accentuated my curves, I looked sensuous yet simple, it was a perfect outfit for the evening.

'You look beautiful, this outfit is just perfect for you, neither too revealing nor does it hides much,' commented Vikram.

'Do we go for this one or should I try the third outfit?' I asked exuberant, my nervousness vanished.

'I don't think you need to try third one, this is perfect blend between casual and formal, I guess you can wear this at office too,' he assured me and turned towards the sales girl, he commanded to her, 'please get me the bill for the two outfits,' he handed over his visa card to her.

'Why are you getting both the outfits packed?' I inquired.

'Well one outfit for you and the other for me,' he informed.

'For you???? I don't think this will suit you,' I mocked Vikram, after being deride by him umpteen number of times, I definitely didn't want to waste the golden opportunity, ' I didn't know you are this types.'

'I mean I want to gift this to some one special on a special occasion,' he said explicably.

'Oh,' a pinch of jealousy played in my eyes.

'And why are you paying for my outfit?' I inquired.

'It's just a dress, take it as a gift from me,' he said.

'I don't accept gifts without occasion, that's illogical,' I informed.

'Well, then take is as my investment on our deal, so it becomes dealogical,' he said emphasising the word dealogical.

'I have heard of dillogical from you, I didn't know dealogical would come up so soon,' the logophile hidden in me spoke out, 'by the way what deal?'

'You forgot? the deal between us?' he made an attempt to remind me.

'Oh yeah, it's just the deal between us, dealogical' I expressed suppressed, depressed and surmised, 'so it's just dillogical between us?' I repeated with hopeful eyes.

'You are pronouncing it wrong, it's not dillogical, it's dealogical, dillogical is a different thing, there's dil or heart involved in it,' he answered while he gathered the shopping bag and swift off the store.

Heart isn't involved between you and me? I wanted to ask him, but something stopped me from doing so.

•••••

#LOVETONICS 6 You don't reveal any thing which is depicting sad or has a depressing side of your life, guys don't want to play as therapist on first date or even on second (you can reveal all your secrets, when he is yours now when he isn't yours, your personal life is none of his business). You will not bring up topics like your past relations and the reason why they failed miserably, in case he brings up the topic, you will just smile and say, 'things didn't work out,' and move on to next topic. You appear like a soft summer breeze for him rather than a damaged and broken piece of mess.'

#LOVETONIC 7 guys don't like girls who dress up sporty and masculine guys want a girl friend and not a boy friend who is actually a girl, so the more feminine a girl behaves the better it goes. The girls who dress up sporty or masculine end up being the guy's best friend rather than being his girl friend.

#LOVETONIC 8 No matter how jealous you feel, never show it to a guy, I difficult for girls to not feel jealous, but you can always pretend. The reason behind this simple rule is, it makes you DIFFERENT from the other girls.

#LOVETONIC 9.1 THIRTY SIX PERCENT OF YOUR PERSONALITY IS YOUR CLOTHES, choose what you wear wisely and make sure that what ever you choose suits you and fits you, it should neither be oversized nor undersized, it should be YOUR size. We guys don't really bother the label behind the dress, but what's important is, the way it looks on you and the way it fits you, the way your outfit defines and enhances your personality; so never fuss about brands, wear any subtle brand of your choice. I call it stupidity when a girl chooses an expensive branded dress which doesn't suits her rather than a not so expensive outfit which does justice to her body. DON'T over do your self, be on the minimal side when it come to accessorizing your outfits the less the better and if you want to convert the better to the best, then keep it feminine; every thing that you choose for you self, make sure that it is feminine.

CHAPTER 9

The Kolkata book house, Mumbai. Office was a huge luxurious glass edifice. We stood in the swanky foyer waiting for Anuvind Khanna, he was already running late with his schedule.

A Maserati Quattroporte has purred up the street and stopped right in front of the glass door. There is something incredible about these gleaming burnished cars, they make you skip a heart beat.

With the effect of the sensors the glass door to the foyer opened and strides out the executives officers, all looking immaculate in dark suits to welcome the panjandrum.

Kartik, Vikram and me with my fractured toe stood freeze, goggling like children as the passenger door of the Maserati opens, a moment later, stride out a man who was probably running in his late fifties or early sixties, he had alopecia light hair, he was wearing a darker shade of grey suit, he was followed by eight other officers one of them was holding a very expensive looking briefcase.

'That's how a million dollar man looks like,' murmured Vikram, 'I wonder what his nephew looks like,' continued Kartik.

•••••

I was sitting in the conference room facing Mr. Anuvind Khanna, five other executives who sat along him. Kartik occupied a seat to my left and Vikram to my right. A man in navy blue suit stood by the end of the table holding a tiny remote control to the projector went on and on without a pause, 'We believe in a logistical formative alliance,' he pursed his lips and his voice was gentle but droning.

I couldn't interpret a single word, hence I mumbled to myself, 'Oh my god what the hell is logistic formative alliance, I wish Kartik had brief me a bit about it, I wish Mr. Anuvind Khanna doesn't comes up with a question for me, well if he does I would pass on it to Kartik or Vikram.' I looked up at Kartik he too seemed nervous but pretended to be confident, I know he is nervous because I'm his best friend and I know that he fidgets with his lighter when he is nervous. I slowly shifted my gaze to Vikram and to my surprise he was not only appearing to be confident but also he appeared to be sanguine and self assured. There was something about Vikram, he was always phlegmatic and nonchalant. He was always one in the among and among in one. I have started to like him.

'I hope you espouse our values,' that was first time Mr. Anuvind Khanna uttered words in the entire meeting, he seemed to be more of a listener rather than a speaker. His voice was deep and effective his repose was as sanguine as Vikram's. 'I have a small request,' continued Mr. Anuvind Khanna, 'on the auspicious event of the merger, I expect a sitar musical performance as a tribute to Goddess Sarasvati.'

●●●●●

On our way back, none of the three of us uttered a word. Vikram was busy driving, Kartik was mindfully contemplating at the busy street, I was peering out of the window, twirling a strand of my hair between my fingers and retired to cogitate.

'I'm amazed,' I managed to break the ice.

'About???' uttered Kartik.

'I'm amazed that Mr. Anuvind Khanna offers a tribute to Goddess Sarasvati.'

Vikram halts the car at the red signal and turns around to answer me, 'Sunanada Khanna was a disciple to Goddess Sarawati, every event in Kolkata book house is initiated with offering a tribute to Goddess Saravati.'

'You know quite a lot,' said Kartik gazing at Vikram.

'Uhm,' Vikram babbled before answering, 'I did A brief research last night.'

I guess it was only me who didn't know any bit about anything.

●●●●

CHAPTER 10

I was disconsolate spending yet another torpid noon at home with my fractured toe. I sat on the window sill, peering down the busy street wondering about Anuvind Khanna (my office life), Subrato (my personal life), Vikram (my advisory board) and so many other thoughts were running simultaneously in my mind.

My soliqueness was soon interrupted by Risha's voice, 'Shona di, loads of work is better than no work for a workaholic like YOU,' she said in a sardonic tone. Her interminable sermon was yet to come, 'Shona di, can't you relax for a few days? Good that the fracture came to you, even God was aware that you would have never taken an off otherwise. Come on, you have a real life beside office and work, why don't you live that life? you have a coffee date on Sunday which is tomorrow, you can add so many things to do, in your 'to do list', you can file your nails for tomorrow, you can get ample sleep so that you are out of dark circles around your eyes which will aid to a fresher look, please see that you don't over sleep or else your eyes will end up looking puffy, you can do this, you can do that,' she went on non-stop, until her phone bleeped to indicate an expectant call from her best friend, Arpita, who was unfortunately confronting a quandary in her love relationship. I personally wanted to express my utmost gratitude to her friend in need, Arpita, for calling up at a bang on accurate time and sparing me from Risha's sermon.

Risha was undoubtedly one of those girls among her friends, who were reminiscent for advices and suggestions at an event of 'critical situation' in their relationship. Risha immaculately managed to draw the grey line between the black and white of good and bad, right and wrong, beneficial and malignant.

I resumed peering out of the window, my phone bleeped unexpectedly to indicate a text received from Vikram, 'hey reach at Cineplex Juhu, see you at Sharp 5,' as soon as I finished reading the text, I was stunned for a moment.

'Why is Vikram calling me at Cineplex?' I asked my self, I mindlessly peered at my cell phone screen and re-read the text a couple of times for my confirmation.

'You are such a dumbo, he is calling you at Cineplex, because he wants to watch a movie with you,' I answered my own self to satiate my inner questionnaire.

'Should I go, or should I decline?' popped out my next concern. Without any realisation, I entered into a sagacious colloquia with my own self, though me and Vikram ceased to share the cold relation which we did earlier, but we still were not pals to hang out for a movie together.

I kept my concerns aside and in a confused state of mind typed a text to reply to him, 'guess you forgot that I can't drive.'

'Have you heard of a word called CAB? Didn't expect this from a logophile like you,' he countered with a text within couple of seconds. I bet his typing speed was far more alacritous than my thinking speed.

'Cab isn't an original word, it is actually derived from the word cabriolet which means a horse carriage in traditional times,' I replied, it was illicit of him to assume that a logophile like me doesn't knows the word cab (huh).

'Forget the word *cab*, I wonder how did a prototype specimen like you came in to the origin, I should talk to your parents about your origin,' he mocked at me. I could already imagine him laughing at my shudder.

'Instead, why don't you talk to your parent about your origin?' I answered perturbed, 'I hope you know that you are your own paradigm.'

'I wish I were lucky enough to talk to my parents,' he replied.

'I'm sure your parents are so irritated by you, that they decided to chuck you out of their life?' I said mindlessly without giving it a thought.

'Yeah, may be, it was easy for them to chuck me out of their life,' he texted, 'forget about my origin, just do as I say, take a cab and reach Cineplex, see you soon, bye,' he was so miffed by me, that he concluded the conversation as soon as he could.

I walked in an oblivious state towards my wardrobe with my confused mind which was occupied by my contradictory thoughts and drafted various assumptions behind Vikram's unforeseen idea of movie outing. While I was surfing my wardrobe in the search of wearing something appropriate for the movie, Risha ambled in my room and headed towards my bookshelf in search of finding something pertinent to read, she was holding the phone close to her ear indicating that she was still on call with her best friend Arpita, her voice raised and infuriated, 'so what if he asked you out for movie, remember that you hate him Arpita,' she said and my ears raised instinctual in a self reflexive mode to hear Risha when I realised that Arpita's diegesis was more or less similar to mine.

I quickly picked up a beige silk kurta, shut my wardrobe and started to eavesdrop on the duo sororal conversation, though I couldn't hear Arpita's end of the conversation, I tried to interpret the situation with what ever negligible data was available to me.

'No Arpita,' said Risha while she picked up the current ADD IT TUDE edition from the book shelf. I stepped in the changing room and left the door slight open so that I don't shut my self from Risha's voice.

'Yes Arpita,' she said, she managed to hodgepodge my book shelf in couple of second whereas on contrary I took hours to organise it in array. I quickly put on the beige Kurta and stepped out of changing room still eavesdropping on their conversation.

'No Arpita,' said Risha, a huge fraction of the conversation was monosyllabic on Risha's end which made it a difficult task of interpretation for me. I stood facing the full length mirror, did my hair and quickly streaked my eyes with kohl pretending myself as if I was unaffected from Risha and Arpita's conversation. I peered at Risha's reflection casted on the full length mirror.

'Listen to me,' finally Risha used a different combination of words which increased the level of my curiosity instead of easing. She rested herself on the mauve bean bag, cradle the phone that was held upstage between her ear and shoulder letting her hands free to hold the magazine by its spine and flip the pages voluntarily, she continued talking when she stopped flipping pages as she reached a particular article and folded the magazine by it's spine, 'Ok, I'll read out an article for you, its an amazingly useful article written by Vikram Khanna,' I vested addendum attention the moment she emphasised Vikram's name, 'he is a very good journo friend of mine, he is an awesome writer, he is very experienced and his writings are very informative,' Risha began to sing Vikram's ballyhoo without intending to pause. *I wanted to yell out loud that, 'Shut up and read the article Risha,' but I kept my mouth shut and pretended as if I wasn't eavesdropping on their conversation.*

'Okay the article goes like this,' she cleared her throat giving ahem it's onomatopoeia before she began to read in a lucid voice. I peered at the full length mirror which casted a perspicuous image of Risha as she began to read out aloud for Arpita.

LOVE IS LIKE HATE, HATE IS LIKE LOVE

Science has proved that LOVE and HATE, the two most intense existing emotions are separated by a very thin invisible and sentimental wall in the human brain. Some of the nervous circuits in the brain responsible for hatred are the same as those that are used during the feeling of romantic love – although love and hate appear to be polar opposites.

The study advertised for volunteers to take part in the research and 20 people were chosen who professed a deep hatred for an individual. Most chose an ex-lover.

Many volunteers developed feeling of love for the one they hated the most, when the two were left alone in suitable circumstances.

It was further found that the hate circuit includes parts of the brain called the putamen and the insula, found in the sub-cortex of the organ. The putamen is already known to be involved in the perception of contempt and disgust. The same putamen and the insula are also both activated by romantic love. This is not surprising. The putamen could also be involved in the preparation of aggressive acts in a romantic context.

A small difference between love and hate appears to be in the fact that large parts of the cerebral cortex associated with judgement and reasoning become de-activated during love, whereas only a small area is deactivated in hate.

This may seem surprising since hate can also be a consuming passion like love. Whereas in romantic love, the lover is often less critical and judgemental regarding the loved person, it is more likely that in the context of hate the hater may want to exercise judgement....'

(When Risha read it out loud for Arpita, I was hauled in confusion, 'is it possible that the spark of hatred between me and Vikram is actually the spark of love????' I asked my self seeking the answer within myself, 'I don't think so, if that is the case, then why is he helping me out with Subrato. I'm sure there is no love thing between me and Vikram. Have I lost my senses how can such a weird thought cross my mind, me and Vikram ??? Definitely no chance,' I tried to help myself out of the dilemma and was waiting for Risha to finish reading the article and come to a conclusion.)

 Risha finished reading and concluded that, 'So Arpita, my opinion is that you should NOT go for the movie.'

She paused briefly to grasp response from the other side of the conversation. So did I.

'Okay, so do what ever you want, don't ask me,' she said and hang the phone furiously.

'Risha, what is wrong with Arpita?' I asked her when she ironically smirked and placed the magazine aside.

'Shona di, Arpita is gone mad,' she replied.

'Why?' I inquired.

'The guy whom she used to hate a lot, has asked her out for movie and she agreed going out with him,' she answered to my query.

'So what is wrong in that? Isn't it a good thing to cease hatred and become friends?' I asked timid.

'Of course Shona di, it is a good thing,' she unexpectedly agreed to me.

'So why don't you want her to go?' I countered with an urge to get an explanation.

'I want her to go,' she said. I was radically confused by her anomalies, her hypothesis indicated a contradictory story than her contention.

'But you advised to her that she shouldn't go,' I asked her bemused.

'Ohhhh, were you listening to the conversation? Well, I forbid her from going because we human have this tendency of doing things which are forbidden, I was just playing with human psychology,' she said and my eyebrows raised seeking an explanation, 'See Shona di, if I would have told her straight to accept and go with this boy, she would have never agreed to go, but when I asked her to decline and forbid her from going, she will definitely want to go, you see, Adam and Eve ate the Apple only because it was forbidden,' she answered. Her explanation to the diegesis was not only mind blowing but it was actually a blow of mind for me.

'You are such a .....' my jaws dropped at her wits and my smirk burst into uncontrollable laughter. Suddenly I felt as if I was surrounded by love gurus.

'Hehehehhehehhe I know I am a ......' she soon joined me in the belly laugh session and the room was filled with our giggles and guffaws. 'By the way, where are you going?' she interrogated noticing me dressed up in my new beige kurta.

'Oh me? uhm hm um,' I babbled and struggled to find a suitable answer to her query and continued with a lie, 'just a bit bored sitting at home, thought of going to near by mall.'

'But your toe is fractured how will you drive?' she raised her concern.

'Have you heard of the word called CAB?' I smirked and left her vicinity to avoid further interrogation from her.

●●●●●

I made my self comfortable on the rear seat of the cab, as the driver took off the speed, my obscure mind wondered about Vikram and his sudden movie plan. I coerced myself to retrograde my thoughts away from him and peered at the gloaming clementine Sun which appeared obfuscate rather than verve to its own contradiction.

I staggered straight to the Cineplex ticket counter paving my way among the arteries of entertainment seeking peeps who stood in a queue to buy movie tickets. Vikram's familiar masculine frame caught my attention, I directed towards him as he stood tall leaning his body weight on the left leg, he was dressed in a yellow polo T-shirt, *I hate that particular shade, by the way I also hate that particular guy who's wearing it.*

'Hey Shona, you are sharp on time,' he waved pointing out his wrist watch when he saw me approaching towards him. He hadn't shaved for the day which made his jaw line appear brawny and overall he looked both *shabby and compelling* at a same juncture of time. '*How the hell does he manage to look so shabby yet so seductive in that shade of puke, also when he isn't even clean shaved? Shona, there is something wrong in you, how can you adore this guy who is wearing a yellow T-shirt and who isn't clean shaved?' I mumbled to myself and made sure that no one around me was listening.*

'Hi,' I answered in monosyllable enmeshing my hair with my fingers and resting a strand behind my ear. I moved my torso step by step ahead as he moved along with the queue until we reached the booth. A geek appearing guy peered at the led screen behind the counter to help the peeps in acquiring their movie tickets.

Vikram handed him cash and said, 'two corner seats please,' I instantly looked up at Vikram with awful eyes, I couldn't digest the fact that he asked me out for a movie despite the fact that we are not even pals, *ok we are pals but we are not movie pals* and to bemuse me further, he happened to book two corner seats??? What does this insinuates? *should I stay or just walk away?* The moment I turned around to walk away, he followed me, he kept the movie tickets in the back pocket of his jeans and peered at me to speak, 'I have a surprise for you.'

I wanted to yell out at him that *corner seats are already a subject of surprise to me? What the hell you have in your mind? Why are you behaving like a jerk?*

'What surprise?' I asked timid.

'Come I'll show you,' he promptly held my hand and dragged me along with him into the elevator, making me numb and flabbergasted.

He got off the elevator which schlepped us on the 2nd floor and walked towards a spa salon which was situated on the left side of the elevator.

'Salon?' I shrugged bemused while I followed him.

'No, it is not just a salon it is your *#LOVETONIC 9.2 TWENTY FOUR PERCENT OF YOUR PERSONALITY IS BEING YOU, BEING YOURSELF remember and repeat a hundred times in your mind that "I am me and that no one can be." Take care of your self because you are the most important person for you. Treat your self with a spa session or just a manicure or any small service at a regular interval of time; the plus point of this love tonic is that when you constantly invest in small effort in your own self, you will not have to invest big effort on the day or a day before your date, also you will end up looking your best always. With being your best I don't mean being flawless or perfectly gorgeous, I mean to give up your slovenliness and be neat, for example a small change like applying a nude lip gloss always will keep your lips moist and full (many such changes occupy a list). Take up an activity of your choice, be it music class; learn the guitar* *or piano, start going to gym or yoga classes, take up an art or painting classes, choose what ever you want, this will keep you happily busy (there is a difference between being busy and being happily busy). The essence of this rule is investing time and love in your own self,'* he answered, 'tomorrow you have a coffee date with Subrato, so I thought you should pamper your self,' he explained as he entered the salon *uhh I mean the spa and the beauty studio.*

'So this is my surprise?' I heaved in relief, 'I thought, well, umm, nothing' I babbled in a state of ambiguous confound, my plastered ankle halted in a sync.

'Okay, did you think that the movie is your surprise?' Vikram said while bursting out into laughter, at times I wondered if he is a mind reader, *such a perfect horrible thought.*

I nodded and said in my defence, 'Come on, you texted me to reach at Cineplex at Sharp 5 so it was a *hypothetical extrapolation,*' I drew out my cell phone and showed the text to him.

'So if I call you at NASA space centre does it interprets that I am taking you to moon?' he never missed a chance to mock at me, 'Heheh Look at yourself, you are *hypothetical extrapolation* as a whole,' he said as he turned away and walked inside the studio

'So who is accompanying you for the movie?' I ignored his mockery and asked the important question as I followed him in the spa studio.

He tousled his hair and said that, 'well, I just thought that when you are busy at the spa pampering and entertaining yourself, why shouldn't I let some one entertain me?' he did not gave a coherent reply to my question.

'I hope the movie entertains you,' I said intrigued still seeking an articulate answer.

'I mean, my definition of *entertainment,*' he explained forming inverted commas in air with his hands over the word *entertain-*

ment.

'I'm glad that I know only one definition of *entertainment*, tell me who are you going with?' *Oh come on name her.*

'Deepika,' he confessed.

Oh! Bicthika, he was going to a movie with bicthika and that too corner seats for the two. To my consternation Bitchika was a masticated chewing gum left without flavour but on contrary he was still ON with her!!!!!

'Okay Deepika,' I said unstirred, I was an amateur in handling such situations where I was in need to hide my jealousy, or may be I was amateur in handling such people, especially bitches.

Vikram turned towards the receptionist and smiled ingeniously, 'I have scheduled a body spa treatment and hair do for my friend Shonali.'

'Please let me check sir,' the receptionist threw an affable red lacquered lips smile to Vikram as she juggled her gaze between the laptop screen and him. 'Sir, please take your seat for a while,' she said pointing out the golden couch placed beside the black Buddha statue. The calm poly-resin fountain head statue was an ideal ornate for the embellishment of salon's interior. Buddha smiled back at me the moment I peered at him.

Vikram occupied a seat beside me as he continued to talk, 'movie begins at 6.00, by that time, I can sit with you and eat your brains,' he said.

'Yeah sure, you can do this job really well,' I mocked Vikram. My phone bleeped to indicate a call from Subrato. The moment I saw Subrato's name flashing on my cell phone screen my sensory organs were rushed with adrenaline, serotonin, oxytocin and all the other hormones which are responsible for making you fall mad for your crush. I sprang off the couch in exuberance, 'that's Subrato calling, Oh my God, he is calling me up, he is calling me up, what do I say, how do I talk?' I squealed in excitement.

'Relax,' instructed Vikram in a firm voice, 'don't take the call, decline it.'

'Noooo, I want to hear his voice,' I announced.

'Just do as I say,' he commanded.

I wrinkled my nose out of dismay and abided with him.

'Now that you have declined the call, type a text for him that you are busy and you will talk to him later,' he instructed to me, 'don't mention details about what are you busy with or when will you talk to him, the lesser details, the better it goes.'

I obeyed Vikram without questioning him because I was already cognizant with his reasoning. Though his logics and laws of love were extreme on both the sides, painful, difficult to follow, old fashioned, at times I was frustrated and contumacious towards his love theory but some thing deep within me started to believe and accept that his theories made perfect sense with the reference to the context.

'Will wait for your text,' my phone bleeped to indicate a text from Subrato, I read it and kept my phone aside without replying to him.

I picked up a Bollywood gossip magazine from the rack and Vikram play fully snatched the magazine from me, he drew out a gel pen from his pocket and started systematically defacing photographs of beautiful people in magazines. He added a moustache onto a leading actress, then inked out a missing tooth. Soon it was an onslaught of scars and eye patches and bloodshot eyes and devil horns until the picture was so ruined that I giggled and laughed till my stomach ached and at the same point of time, Vikram's phone bleeped to indicate a text from *Bitchika*, she had arrive and it was time for Vikram to leave.

He kept his phone in the pocket after reading the text and turned toward me to command, 'listen, call me once you are done, I'll drop you home, I'm a staircase away.'

'No, I am well aware of the word CAB,' I denied politely.

'Don't be a fool, gimme a call, I'll drop you,' he said as he stood up to leave.

'No I'll be fine,' I behaved stubborn and feigned a sardonic smile. I ignored an incomprehensible deluge of jealousy which swamped inside me when it was about Vikram and Bitchika (or any other girl replacing Bitchika.)

'I'm running out of time for an argument, just do as I say, I'll see you, bye,' he said and left my vicinity within seconds leaving me intrigues with the thought that *why did he demand to see me after the spa session?*

●●●●●

I changed into a fluffy white bath robe which had the spa's logo; two self coloured doves embroidered on the left and as I slipped my feet on to the boat shaped white bath slippers, I realised that the slippers were so soft and comfortable for my plastered toe that I should have replaced my floaters with them on the very same day I got the plaster. I went in to the tiny room which smelled like fresh lavender, instrumental melody played in the background.

Spa treatment worked as an extravagant tranquilizer not only for my body but also for my mind. I was coddled with aromatic lavender oil and coated with mud pack, every nerve in my body was soothed with profusion of serendipity. I was mentally hauled to alpine meadows in early summer as the multitude of floral bliss aroma were reaching at the peak my olfactory perfection. As the dermatologist moved her fingers over my face in a upward direction a gentle breeze wafting the scent into my nose and my head spins with remarkable intoxication. I was grateful to Vikram for the wonderful surprise. *Although I didn't want to think about him at that pacifying moment,* my mind wandered in his direction. *He must be busy watching movie with Bitchika,are they really watching movie or....?? So what if they are not watching movie or doing whatever....* I was over reacting, or was I jealous? may be we girls are always jealous, jealousy is in our nature, would I be jealous if Subrato goes out with another girl or was my jealousy restricted to Vikram and Bitchika. I reined my thoughts and instantly focused onto the calming spa treatment. I shifted my gaze at the cast plaster, how desperately I desiderate that my feet was out of cast band aid so that my pro-tuberance wasn't devoid of the indulging experience.

'Take off my cast plaster,' I don't know what took into me, but I wanted to get rid of my cast plaster, I didn't want to drag it any more with me. It was just a slight toe fracture and I wasn't feel-ing any pain, I knew I was fine.

'What?' asked the dermatologist.

'Please get me rid of my cast plaster,' I repeated.

'Are you sure ma'am?' she asked to confirm.

'100 percent positive,' I confirmed.

She left the tiny room and returned with a big sharp scissors to get me rid off my plaster.

A hair do session was waiting for me which was coeval scheduled to be followed by the extravagant spa treatment. I followed the hair stylist as she headed towards the hair section of the salon, I occupied a seat on a hydraulic recliner chair facing the full length mirror and I was stunned for a moment to see my reflection on the casting surface, my skin was rubicund glowing with the effect of the spa treatment. I couldn't wait any further to avail a new coiffure so that I could get a glimpse of my rejig appearance.

I had my hair washed, after my cosmologist wrapped a water proof apron around my shoulders and tied it to the nape, despite I tried without success to explain I had thoroughly washed my curls that morning, I was informed by the cosmologist that during the wash she would be adding specially formulated conditioner to give my hair more volume and the emollients would help in making the scalp softer, then my hair would be styled while it was wet.

As her scissors were furiously clicking and the resulting bushels of hair were gently floating on the floor, I was worried about retaining the long length of my hair, *after all I am a Bengali and I'm concerned about the length of my hair*, I crossed my finger and looked away from the mirror to avoid perturbing myself any further. I shifted my gaze to contemplate at the aisles of expensive maquillage and cosmetic products arranged in a series of ascending order with respect to their heights, I realised how little I was cognizant with modern body and hair care regimes, my previous visits to claustrophobic salons were restricted to eyebrows threading were archaically different from this particular surprise gift pampering session from Vikram. I continued to scan the salon, a huge poster concealed the wall which read;

Small changes that can make big difference;

● Salons offer a wide range of permanent hair straightening treatments, go for one, it is easy to wake up to straight an manageable hair. Grow your hair longer.

● Keep your nails filed and coat them with a nude shade of paint.

● Take ample rest so that you don't get dark circles.

● Go for a walk or jog or take up any physical activity or a sport of your choice.

• Meditate for a glowing skin rather than investing money in expensive cosmetics products.

• Find cheap natural home alternates to expensive creams and toiletries in your kitchen.

• Your day is as long as 24 hours, spare an hour for your self in silence and solitude.

• Smell good always.

• BUY one outfit/pair of foot wear which suits you rather than buying ten. Choose wisely.

• Give up bad habit like smoking and drinking. (You are a future mom to his children, do you want your children to smoke and drink like you do?) Ask your self.

• Volunteer for an N.G.O.

• Believe and listen to your instinct, they never lie.

• Always smile.

As I concluded reading the informative piece, the cosmologist took off my apron when she finished her job of truncating my bangs of hair, I excitedly stood up and promptly looked up at myself on the mirror!!!!!! That was a brand new ME, who looked straight into my eyes with confidence and a zygomatic smile. I was already in love with my new coiffure, my hair were straight *not pin straight but fluffy and bouncy straight*, the layered bangs begun at my cheek bones and ran down at a point between my chin and neck. To add on to my astonishment, the length of my hair wasn't very short.

To my dejection, time passed expeditiously and the palliative episode came to an end. I drew out my phone from my bag and typed THANK YOU in caps lock with an intention to express my gratitude to Vikram, but promptly I backspaced, probably because I didn't want to disturb him while he was busy with Bitchika entertaining himself in the movie. I preclude myself and postpone the thanks giving. I stepped out of the salon into *reality* and booked a cab to hail back home, using the relevant app from my smart phone as I got off the elevator and staggered towards the street.

A car drove in high speed, slipped and stopped right in front of me. I was bemused for a moment until; the glass window shield rolled down and a familiar voice spoke, 'I told you to call me as soon as you finish,' that was Vikram's sonorous voice, he never happened to miss a negligible chance to baffle me.

'I didn't want to disturb you and Deepika,' I said.

'Come, sit in the car,' he commanded an invitation.

'I have called for a cab, it must be arriving soon,' I answered.

'Cancel the cab,' he switched off the ignition and stepped out of the car.

'That's nugatory, cab is already on its way and I don't want to pay unnecessary cancellation charges,' I denied accepting his suggestion.

Vikram said nothing but snatched my phone off my hand and cancelled the cab, 'I told you to let me know when you are done with the spa treatment, why didn't you inform me?' he walked towards the other side of the car and opened the door to the passenger seat for me.

'How did you know that I'm done with the spa?' I walk past by car towards him, stood facing him and shut the door that he held and countered my question instead of answering his.

Vikram relaxed his body folded his arm and leaned his body weight on the gas guzzler, 'I am well cognizant with your stubborn behaviour, I knew you would never inform me, so I told the receptionist to do the need,' he quenched my query.

'And she agreed so easily?' I demanded to know, I stood beside him leaning my body weight on the bonnet of his car.

'Of course, I gave her *something* in return,' he said.

'What is in reference in context to your *something*?' I asked snooping.

'My phone number. You don't know the importance of my phone number, girls are willing to kill and die for Vikram Khanna's number.'

I said nothing but smirked at his flamboyancy.

'Come let's go,' he once again opened the door to the passenger seat for me and I popped in promptly.

     Vikram occupied his seat in the car, turned on the ignition and drove off swiftly.

'You are looking nice,' he smirks, 'I wanted to see you after the spa session so that I could see the work which salon did on you, I must say, they did a great job.'

Oh! so that was the sole reason behind his aberrant need to see me after the spa session.

'Thanks, how was the movie?' I asked.

'I don't know how was it, Deepika and me were too busy to watch the movie,' he notified giving a notorious smile. 'So you are all set for tomorrow, is he picking you up?' he asked after a brief pause.

'Who?' I inquired oblivious.

'Subrato,' he enlightened. *I almost forgot about Subrato.*

'I don't know if he will pick me up,' I shrugged insouciantly.

'Didn't you reply after that last text?' he demanded to know.

'Nope, I was busy enjoying the spa session' I answered pococurante.

'Holy shit and you are telling me now?' he impetuously applied break to the car and the force of inertia propelled my body weight in a forward direction, his impromptu respond to stimulus gave a sharp jerk to the car.

'Why have you stopped spontaneously here right in front of this ice cream parlour?' I asked.

'To treat you with an ice-cream,' he said sarcastically.

'Oh that's so sweet of you, first the spa then the ice cream thank you so much for all this,' I answered unaware of his sarcasm.

'YOU ARE HOPELESS,' he said emphasising each word, his eyes filled with agitation.

'What do you mean?' I folded my arms in an akimbo out of vexation.

'You dumbo, tomorrow you have a coffee date with Subrato and you don't even know whether he will pick you or no and all you are concerned is about ice cream,' he said in a raised intonation to make me realise that I was actually dumb.

'So what? I am a grown up girl, I can go by my self and I know the meaning of the word cab,' I answered in a pretence, as if I don't care, but I really really really do care.

'You fool, he might have never put up that effort for any girl in past so if he comes to pick you up that will leave him shocked and amazed on his own behaviour, he will spend hours wondering that he ought to see you so much that he choose to drive all the way to pick you up,' he said explicably.

'Oh,' I didn't agree with him completely but I didn't disagree either.

'And we will make him pick you up from your place,' he said confidently.

'How?' I asked timid.

'Leave a forwarded message for him,' he commanded to me. 'Now, this forwarded message will work as a HELLO, a girl should not text a HELLO or a HI at an initial stage of a relationship, so be wise and drop an appropriate forwarded message.'

'Which message?' I inquired.

'Any forwarded message like a forwarded joke or a suggestive message or an informative message, any message in your inbox,' he suggested.

I opened my whatsapp messenger and scrolling down to find out a few forwarded messages; 'ten ways to keep your weight in check, twenty reasons to take up a healing and meditation classes, understand GST,' I shifted my gaze away from phone and looked up at him, ' I think I should forward this message, understand GST, it is an informative piece.'

'Oh God, please give me strength to deal with this girl!!!!' his voice filled with agitation and vexation, 'wait a second I'll forward you a joke, you pass it on to him,' he opened his whatsapp messenger and soon forwarded a text.

My phone beeped and I opened it to read a very adulterous joke forwarded by Vikram, 'Haaawww this joke is not good, it is pathetic,' I covered my mouth with my hands in an awww and smothered a giggle.

'If it's not good it wouldn't have made you smile,' he debated.

'I mean it's dirty, I can't forward this to him, what will he think of me?' I raised my concern.

'If you cant forward it, I'll do it,' he snatched my phone successfully dodged me and forwarded the text before I could grab my phone back from his clasp.

Vikram peacefully handed over the phone to me while I burst my balloon of anger on him, 'How could you do this Vikram, what do you think of yourself?' I said perturbed and I suddenly smiled while my phone bleeped and received a text from Subrato. 'Oh my God, it is a reply from Subrato, let me check what he says,' I nervously opened messenger to read the message received, ' he says *hi*, just a plain *hi*, couldn't he say something else?' I kept my phone aside in dismay.

'What else do you expect from a boring Bengali doctor hehehe?' mocked Vikram, while he reignited the car and resumed to drive towards my home.

I glared at him while he vested his concentration on driving.

'Okay, you have to behave with Subrato in the same manner you behave with the guys you don't really like, or you are not really interested in,' he suggested.

'But I like him and I am interested in him,' I confessed.

'#LOVETONIC 10 *Have you ever figured it out that the guys who keeps on calling a girl or trying on a girl is the guy who has actually realised that the girl is not an easy task for him or probably she has turned him down, thus the girl becomes a challenge for the guy, the boy strives as hard as he can to get her. So the moral of the story is YOU HAVE TO BECOME THAT CHALLENGE FOR SUBRATO. Have you ever noticed why do boys like sports more than girls like sports? Why do guys download and play more games than girls do? The simple reason behind this behaviour of boys is that we men like challenges, so you have to be that challenge for Subrato ,'* he explained, 'Type a text for him as I dictate,' Vikram initiated to dictate as I typed, '*Hello Dr. Subrato, the joke which you just now received was sent to you mistakenly, I came out for an ice cream with a very old friend of mine and he happened to be in a mischievous mood, so while he was fidgeting with my phone, he sent it to you, I am ex-*

tremely sorry for his behaviour, good night,' the text was formal.

No sooner did I sent the text than I received a reply from Subrato, it read as, 'which friend?' I read it out for Vikram in a demand to know my next step.

'Tell him, just a friend, nothing serious,' Vikram instructed and I obediently followed his instructions he took a sharp left turn as we almost reached my home.

'Okay,' replied Subrato.

'Huh, he replied with just an OK, he hasn't yet told me that he would pick me up,' I kept my phone aside and turned towards Vikram to reveal my dejection.

'Reply with a smiley,' said Vikram.

'Why only a smiley?' I inquired Vikram as we arrived my home and he turned off the ignition of the car.

'Well, if a guy is really interested in you, he will reply to your stupid smileys, monosyllables and every nonsense,' Vikram shared the piece of his knowledge with me. He applied brake to his car to halt at the porch of my home, I looked up at Risha's window, the lights were still on indicating that Risha wasn't asleep yet.

The moment I was getting off the car, my phone beeped to indicate a text from Subrato, 'I'll pick you up tomorrow at sharp 6.'

I was stunned for a moment or two, I couldn't help my self but I looked up at Vikram with utmost bewilderment and I was amazed that he exactly knew Subrato's response, because when Vikram asked me to mention that I was hanging around with a friend in ice cream parlour, indirectly, he incepted insecurity in Subrato's mind. Boys are allergic to insecurity.

'Vikram,' I squealed out loud in excitement, 'he said he will come to pick me up,' I announced as I exit the car and he followed me out to breath in some fresh air.

'I knew it, tell him, don't bother your self, I'll manage,' said Vikram as he leaned on the bonnet of his car at the parking spot around my home.

'No, I don't want to tell him a NO,' I leaned on the car, beside him.

'Do as I say Shona,' he insisted.

I started to type, 'I'll manage, please don't bother your self,' and I tabbed on the send icon.

'Don't be silly, I'll pick u up ,' appeared Subrato's reply.

'hm,' I said.

'Great,' replied Subrato.

'Gn,' I said and exit the whatsapp messenger, before he makes an exit.

'Gn,' he replied after my exit.

I turned towards Vikram and raised my both the hands in the air to bow him, 'You are a dating guru Vikram,' I praised him, he didn't say anything but looked up at my illuminated face, he was happy to see me happy, 'oh my God, I am feeling so .....' a logophile like me struggled to find appropriate word to describe my feeling,

'You are feeling nervous and excited at a same point of time,' clarified Vikram.

'Yes,' I nodded a yes.

'And you feel something tingly in your stomach, popularly called as butterflies,'

'Exactly,' I abided.

'That's called collywobbles Miss. Logophile.'

'Perfecto,' I said, Subrato's text transported me to cloud nine, 'but I'm so nervous Vikram, what will I talk? How will I talk? How will I behave? Do you know I'm a very shy person? how will I manage Vikram ?' he looked at me and smiled at my madness.

'So here come the #LOVETONIC *9.3 THIRTY SIX PERCENT OF YOUR PERONALITY IS THE WAY YOU BEHAVE your deportment is the attitude that you carry along with yourself. The way you sit, the way you look at him (never stare, make an eye contact but keep the staring part to the minimal), the way you walk (walk as if you are the Greek goddess of love who has just landed on earth. Move around with modesty keeping your back straight and pass a swift brisk walk), the way you smile demurely, the way you talk (maintain a high level of politeness in your speech and voice when you address the waiter or any other personnel around you) and the most important part, the last but not the least is the way you listen to him, (listening to him patiently has plus points; when you listen more you obviously talk less, also when you listen you can observe him and connect the points with the reflection of his words and you are able to draw a more vivid and clear conclusion about his personality.) You will not accept or abide with things which your heart doesn't agrees just to please him, say for example if Subrato brings up a political or a social topic which you don't accept or abide with, you will never lie or pretend to abide with it. May be your disagreeing behaviour will arise a debatable conversation but be happy that you are being honest with your self. I am not asking you to be rude or to fight to put up your point, I am just asking you to politely stand for what you feel is right. At the same time don't feel dismayed if he doesn't accepts your point of view, understand that it's perfectly fine if he doesn't accepts your perception, every one has their own perception, so does he, don't expect from him to change his perception but also don't compromise on your ideas and principles. Be YOU Shonali, be authentic to your ownself, he should fall in love with YOU. These love tonics are not only about to attract a guy or make him fall in love with YOU, but it is more about loving your ownself and unfolding a better version of*

YOU. YOU are a girl with self esteem and self worth, YOU don't chase guys. YOU are YOU.'

'This sounds great,' I admitted. 'should we rehearse? Why don't you pretend to be Subrato and I'll pretend to be Shonali,' I smack on my forehead for being dumb and rectified my self, 'I mean, I am Shonali, I don't need to pretend to be Shonali, Uff!!! I am talking rubbish, see I am so nervous, please help me out by rehearsing.'

I stood up and stared at Vikram for longer than a minute, he too contemplated me.

He said nothing while I was still waiting for him to talk.

'Say something,' I uttered after a long impede.

'What do I say?' he asked half smile.

'Say anything, you have dated so many girls in past, you always know exactly what to say and what to do,' I said.

'Yes, I have dated many girls,' his voice calm and sensual, 'but I have never been on a date with some one like you,' he confessed, his eyes empty and covetous, he leaned in and came extremely closer to me, he smelled like fresh cologne, perfume; his musk tinged my nostrils. His deep revealing eyes fixated on me were shining with strange astonishment. Was he about to kiss me? Did he wanted to kiss me? Or was I expecting to be kissed by him? My body was vibrating with anticipation of questions and answers. The air between us grew intense, there was a sudden shift in his behaviour, Before I could comprehend his behaviour, he came even more closer and whispered in my left ear, 'Shonali, I guess you left your floaters in the salon, you are still wearing the dove imprinted bath slippers,' I instantly shifted my gaze towards my feet and we burst out in laughter over my stupidity.

'How did you forget your floaters in the salon?' Vikram stopped laughing and demanded to know the reason behind my illicit behaviour.

I said nothing but shrugged in response to his question.

Vikram unlocked the door to the driver's seat of his car, quickly occupied his seat and drove off the street vanishing in the dark night within seconds.

•••••

#RULE 9.3 THIRTY SIX PERCENT OF YOUR PERONALITY IS THE WAY YOU BEHAVE your deportment is the attitude that you carry along with yourself. The way you sit, the way you look at him (never stare, make an eye contact but keep the staring part to the minimal), the way you walk (walk as if you are the Greek goddess of love who has just landed on earth. Move around with modesty keeping your back straight and pass a swift brisk walk), the way you smile demurely, the way you talk (level of politeness in your speech and voice when you address the waiter or any other personnel around you) and the most important part, the last but not the least is the way you listen to him, (listening to him patiently has plus points; when you listen more you obviously talk less also, when you listen you can observe him and connect the points with the reflection of his words and you are able to draw a more vivid and clear conclusion about his personality.)

Be proud of your achievements. You will not accept or abide with things which your heart doesn't agrees just to please a guy say for example if Subrato bring up a political or a social topic which you don't accept or abide with, you should never lie or pretend to abide with it, have an opinion of your own. May be your disagreeing behaviour will arise a debatable conversation but be happy that you are being honest with your self. I am not asking you to be rude or to fight to put up your point, I am just asking you to politely stand for what you feel is right. At the same time don't feel dismayed if he doesn't accepts your point of view, understand that it's perfectly fine if he doesn't accepts your perception, every one has their own perception, so does he, don't expect to change his perception but also don't compromise on your ideas and principles. Be YOU Shonali, he should fall in love with YOU. These rules are not only about to attract a guy or make him fall in love with YOU, but it is more about loving your own self and unfolding a better version of YOU. YOU are a girl with self esteem and self worth, YOU don't chase guys. YOU are YOU.

#LOVETONIC 10 Have you ever figured it out that the guys who keeps on calling a girl or trying on a girl is the guy who has actually realised that the girl is not an easy task for him or probably she has turned him down, thus the girl becomes a challenge for the guy, so the boy strives as hard as he can to get her. So the moral of the story is YOU HAVE TO BECOME THAT CHALLENGE FOR THAT BOY. Have you ever noticed why do boys like sports more than girls like sports? Why do guys download and play more games than girls do? The simple reason behind this behaviour of boys is that men like challenges, so you have to be that challenge rather than being easily available.

•••••

CHAPTER 11

It was THE DAY, I woke up to bright sun light and Vikram's text which read as, 'good morning Shona, reach office in an hour.'

I sat up on the bed and rubbed my eyes gently, I typed a reply to his text, 'today is Sunday, who works on Sunday?' I checked for the few other notifications as I opened the window curtain to view calm morning sun and occupied a place to sit on the window sill.

My phone beeped to indicate a text received, 'I agree nobody works on Sunday, but I guess Bengal tigress's toe is better so she got rid of the plaster yesterday at the salon. We have loads of pending work, so see soon you at office.' I read the text and resumed peering out at the clementine sun.

I typed in a reply, 'but I'm busy today, you already know that I have plans for evening with Subrato, (the most awaited coffee date.)'

'That is in the evening Shona, stop showing tantrums and reach office soon,' he replied, I couldn't grasp his anomalous behaviour.

'Are you ordering me? I'm your boss and not vice versa,' I replied agitated.

'I'm not ordering you, I'm doing what I have been told to do, Kartik wants you in office today so he told me to inform you,' he clarified.

'Okay see you at office in an hour,' I dismissed our conversation without arguing any further.

●●●●●

In office, where Kartik, Vikram, Bitchika, Amrita and Pranay were already present in the conference room.

'Here Shonali is!!!' exclaimed Kartik as he saw me approaching the conference room through the glass door, 'what took you so long?' he inquired as I entered, 'anyway take your seat,' he pointed a seat next to him before I could answer his question.

'Kartik why are we here in office on Sunday? Is there some problem?' I asked as I occupied my seat.

'Well, Vikram has something great to announce,' the glint in his eyes indicated that the urgent Sunday meeting wasn't a leitmotif of problem.

Vikram stood up confidently, every eyes in the conference room fixated on him while he proceeded towards the projector and started to speak in his casual swagger tone,' hey guys, how you all doing? I know you guys are pissed off and I'm sure one of you wants to kill me right away because I scheduled this meeting on Sunday morning,' he continued as he looked up at me, 'but I have a wonderful news for us,' his voice was filled with excitement and exuberance, 'MODE DE VIE is not only taking us global but also ADD IT TUDE and MODE DE VIE are jointly coming up with a new product which is #LOVETONICS,' Vikram uttered out each word with his maximum zeal and passion, he contemplated me for the entire tenure of time while he was making the announcement.

A gust of excitement tab through the room, every body stood up and hi-fied each other in response, 'Woho, this is amazing news, I'm so happy Kartik,' I walked a step towards

Kartik and half hugged him, Pranay squealed in excitement and jumped, his over weight body gave a mini earthquake to the edifice. Bitchika deliberately hugged Vikram tightly. I was totally pissed of her coquette deportment where as Vikram excused him self and stood beside me meeting his gaze with mine, he half smiled, last night's weirdness and awkwardness was still present in the air between Vikram and me.

Every one present in the room was extremely happy, Kartik continued to speak as every one settled down, 'And the credit goes to Vikram and Shonali, you two are great together,' I looked up at Vikram in response to the appreciation to find that he was already contemplating at me and half smiling.

'That is all Vikram's effort, his love tonics are awesome.' I praised him and left the conference room in a hurry, I rushed in to my cabin and started to organise my things. My cabin had become Hodge podge since I was on a leave for previous few days.

Vikram followed me in to my cabin and said, 'Congratulation Shona.'

'To you too Vikram,' I smirked, I piled up all the files in a series and kept them aside.

'You look disturbed,' Vikram inquired as he helped me in clearing my table, he kept the stray pens in the pen holder, cleared petty things.

'Oh, no, I'm just a bit nervous, I had other plans for today. I just wanted to do nothing before Subrato came in to pick me up, but I guess your announcement couldn't wait until tomorrow?' my table was cleared.

'Of course I could have wait until tomorrow but I purposely wanted to keep you occupied today,' said Vikram.

I said nothing but shrugged and gave him a worried glance.

'Relax you need #LOVETONIC 11,' Vikram made me sit on the

chair and occupied the opposite seat, he continued to speak, '*#LOVETONIC 11 is KEEP YOURSELF BUSY BEFORE THE DATE. You girls have a tendency to shrink your world for THAT particular guy, you always talk about him to your girlfriends, think of him and you want to involve him in everything you do. Why do you girls forget that you had a life of your own before he came in and you have a life of your own when he is in and you will continue to have this life of your own whether he will or will not be in it. He is just a part of your life not your life as whole. The time before the date should be your own time, try to keep your self busy until your door bell rings. This rule will not let your mind wander all day in his direction, it will help you behave normal and keep your self from being nervous, plus, your world doesn't shrinks. The logic behind this rule is; when you are occupied all day before the date, you don't give yourself any time to think about the date. various questions don't bother you, questions like what will you talk, how will you talk, when will you react, doesn't bother you. When your mind isn't under the influence of such questionnaire, you are yourself and you behave normal.*'

'Wow this is cool, trust me, I'm loving each and every #LOVETONIC,' I appreciated.

He winked playfully and said, 'I would suggest that ask him to pick you from office.'

'But my outfit, the one which we bought for the date, its at home,' I raised my concern.

'I'll ask Risha to drop it in the office,' he came up with a solution.

'Great, I'll text Subrato to pick me up from office,' I said as I piled up waste paper and put them into the bin and excused myself.

•••••

#LOVETONIC 11 is KEEP YOURSELF BUSY BEFORE THE

DATE. You girls have a tendency to shrink your world for THAT particular guy, you always talk about him to your girl friends, think of him and you want to involve him in everything you do. Why do you girls forget that you had a life of your own before he came in and you have a life of your own when he is in and you will continue to have this life of your own whether he will or will not be in it. He is just a part of your life not your life as whole. The time before the date should be your own time, try to keep yourself busy until your door bell rings. This rule will not let your mind wander all day in his direction, it will help you behave normal and keep your self from being nervous, plus, your world doesn't shrinks. The logic behind this rule is; when you are occupied all day before the date, you don't give yourself any time to think about the date. various questions don't bother you, questions like what will you talk, how will you talk, when will you react, doesn't bother you. When your mind isn't under the influence of such questionnaire, you are your self and you behave normal.'

CHAPTER 12

Subrato leaned for support over the bonnet of his car while he was waiting for me. He appeared inordinately handsome in a white shirt and nice blue denim, there was something vital and strong about him, a physicality of depth that set him off apart the other men I was dating previously. He looked up at me with a sharp chiselled grin, 'God!!!!! Finally you are here Shonali, I was hoping that I won't have to spend my entire life at this spot, outside the office of this beautiful Bengali girl waiting for her,' Subrato's eyes flickered as he addressed to me with an abstract.

'I'm amazed that you are a mind reader along with being a doctor, how come you are aware of my plan to keep you waiting for me,' I replied in a whimsical sense to tease him.

A broad smile danced on his lips and his eyes glittered, 'it would be an honour to wait for a gorgeous girl like you,' he said, he courteously opened the door to the passenger seat of the car.

Did he just compliment me? Oh yes Shona he did. Am I behaving as per #LOVETONICS? Yes Shona you are. Am I authentic to myself? Yes Shona you are. Should I say something more? Should I stay quiet and just smile? Various such thoughts played hide and seek in my mind, I was trying to appear confident from outside, but I was feeling doltish and edgy on my inside. Chronicle of love tonics were running in my mind sequentially and I was constantly nudged by my thoughts.

'Thanks,' I kept my words minimal and occupied the seat in the car.

Subrato drove swiftly as I peered outside the window, 'Shonali,' he alluded softly.

'Yes,' I responded.

'I want you to meet some one,' he said.

'Some one???' I inquired with suspicion. *Does he wants me to meet his mom or sister? Oh come on Shona who does that on first date. May be, he already has a girlfriend and he wants me to meet her, or may be ex girlfriend? Shona nobody does that either on a first date. OMG I'm so confused and nervous. If magically, a genie appeared and asked me for a wish to be granted, I would have asked for invisible presence of Vikram through out my date, so that he could guide me on all my assumptions, suppositions and contradictions.*

'Some one who will make your day,' Subrato's gentle voice hauled me back to reality from the fragile world of my assumptions and suppositions, 'her name is Lily, she is waiting for you at the back seat,' said Subrato peering ahead, as he steered the steering wheel with his right hand and his left hand rested on the gear lever shifter.

I promptly turned around to scrutinise, 'Oh! These are lovely,' I warmly picked up the bouquet of Lily flowers and chuckled bedazzled by his effort.

'Thanks Subrato, that's a lovely gesture,' I thanked him profusely staying equipoised. More than the flowers, I loved the way he offered them to me, he transpired to be plain and simple guy with a twist of percipient interpretation to impress a girl.

I promptly texted Vikram and told him that, 'the geek Bengali doctor isn't really boring, he has a fun romantic element hidden in him.'

Soon appeared Vikram's reply, 'may be, he too has prepared himself with love tonic's version for boys to impress you, but I bet you he can't have a fun element hidden in him,' I rolled my eyes in response to his reply, switched off my phone and kept it in my bag to avoid any further distraction.

'There is some one else too waiting for you in the dashboard storage,' Subrato said pointing out towards the car dashboard storage box.

'Who?' I inquired skittish as I opened the storage box.

'Mr. Rocher,' he answered.

A tiny pack of Ferraro Rocher was waiting for me, 'wow, I love chocolates, thank you so much, but you have to help me in finishing them.

'As far as I know girls, they don't share chocolates, you are generously an exception,' he said as he took a sharp left turn.

'I have a different perception. Why should I alone put on extra weight, the culprit should also be the victim,' I said pointing out to him.

Time flew with Subrato, we reached the destination sooner than ever, it seem that path had shrink. He halts and parks at the parking area of grandeur 'Sea Rock lounge'. The intimacy between the lounge and the sea was amorous, the two were neither very close to each other nor too far away, yet craved for each other. Both adored the panoramic view of each other and longed to be together, its serene locus made it an ideal nest for couples. The interior of the lounge was divided into three: a restaurant, a bar area and the cafe, which was inspired by Caribbean island style of interior, cool pastel shades played on the walls, no paintings adorned the wall; the picturesque view of Arabian sea through massive windows was all the art work cafe needed. Huge Tahiti palm leaf paddle ceiling fans hanged on the ceiling. Seating layout in the cafe was divided in to two; a portion had comfortable lounge for patrons flowing in groups, while other portion was 'table for two' for idyllic couples.

Subrato reserved a table for us by the window bay, the sun was setting and we made it there on the perfect time. Perfect place, perfect timing, perfect partner, everything seem perfect.

'This sunset, this clementine sky, this sun kissing the sea, the calm breeze, this entire view is incredible, this place is beautiful, thank you so much for choosing this place,' I admired the enchanting place in a series.

'Thank you so much for coming with me, it's been ages that I have been here, especially at this hours, I don't remember when did I witness a sunset last,' he expressed.

'Work must be keeping you busy?' I asked.

'Yeah, work and other things in a row. Anyway, how was your day? You are working on weekend, was it a hectic weekend?' he asked concerned.

'No, not at all, it wasn't at all hectic. In fact it was filled with an exciting news,' I said. The older version of Shonali (the one who doesn't knows love tonics) would have blurted out every possible small details about the ADD IT TUDE going global, about how Vikram, Kartik and me are excitedly looking forward for the deal, but thanks to #LOVETONIC 2: talk less talk sense, ran across my mind and I decided to keep details on the minimal side, which provided Subrato with basic data about me and my work.

'How was your day?' I asked as I picked up the menu card to scrutinise it.

'Well, my day was a bit hectic, actually I am working on a new social media connective application which is different from other social media apps, sites and....,' his gleaming eyes were witness of his deep interest in software and systems, he continued, 'did I mention to you that, apart from being an orthopaedic, I have immense passion for software applications, in fact it will interest you to know I'm working on developing a new software.'

'That's impressive, but how many apps do we need to connect to same number of friends?' I commented.

'This is something new and different,' Subrato excitedly went on explaining to me about the new software system which he was developing. Even though I couldn't interpret a single word about the coding, programming, miscellaneous topics related to software development, I was impressed by his multi talent demeanour. He spoke admirably in a series, his eyes were deep, intense and responsive, every thing about him was amorous, his chiselled physiognomy, his movements, the tone of his voice, especially when he laughed, he had a masculine frankness and spontaneity. He indulged while he talk in abundant restlessness rather affected gestures to make me take things in a peculiar way and supreme sense, I was lost in him.

Waiter arrived to take our orders which got a pause to Subrato's monologue, 'A cuppa chino for me and .....' Subrato placed his order and turned towards me to ask mine, 'What will you have Shonali?'

'I'll have a fresh lime soda please,' I placed my order with utmost politeness and smiled generously at the waiter, recalling Vikram's #LOVETONIC 5

'Order something to eat, I'm hungry,' demanded Subrato.

'I don't really have an appetite to eat at this point of time, but how bout we share a piece of chocolate tart?' I asked him for his opinion.

'Chocolate tart is perfect,' he said.

Perfect and aphrodisiac too

'Getting back to the software system I was telling you......' he continued, a small part of me wanted to judge him on being a geek and talkative on the very first date but I recalled *#LOVET-ONIC 12 don't be judgemental or decisive on first date, may be he over talks out of excitement or may be he doesn't talks at all or talks on the minimum side out of nervousness. First date is less about the content and more about the behaviour. Observe his behaviour rather than focusing on the content of his talks. Grasp his perception and put up your perception clearly.*

'Don't you think that this technology, applications, software systems, social media is cutting off the quality in our life?' I put up my point straight considering #LOVETONIC 9.2

Subrato uttered, 'No, I don't think so, on contrary I believe, apps have made things easier, you can take the example of the new application which I am working on....'

I interrupted him and said, 'we assume that social media is helping us but the reality is that people don't seem enough for themselves these days.' I placed my perception and continued in one direction, 'people condense feelings into gifs, no one has time to express feelings by using real words. People scroll down mindlessly their Instagram and Facebook, killing their precious time, liking and following pictures of people they don't even know personally. Each addition to the number of likes on filtered photographs increase the level of adrenaline and dopamine, but have they asked themselves do they like themselves the way they are? We, the people of this generation, are fortunate enough to have a quick access to abundant of free information available on internet, still we are missing the real wisdom, the real essence of life. All we are bothered about is, flaunting our trendy designer outfits, but we forget that there are people out, who don't even have clothes to wear. We crave real connection with virtual friends and fake our feeling with real ones, the true spirit of friendship is lost in this game of hide and seek. We are always busy, it sounds cool to say 'hey I'm busy' or I'm sorry I have been busy' when its time to catch up with real friends, have we asked ourselves, where are we busy? We are not clear with our goals, purpose of life, strategies and plans about life because we are so much interested in what others are doing in their life. And you say social media makes life easier? It's not that I'm an anti social media but anything particularly used in overdose is something which kills you from inside, it makes you hollow from inside,' I kept my point specific, I excused myself to the ladies room and gently swift with a tranquil smile.

In ladies room, I stood facing the mirror amazed at my own self, 'Oh my god, did I speak too much, Vikram warned me, but I just, I just blurted out things in a flow, I didn't want to sound against social media or against the app he is designing, but......... but what Shona? You spoke a lot. No I didn't, I just kept my point straight, vivid and clear, I said what I actually feel for social media,' I argued with my ownself in solitude. 'OMG, I already ruined things with this guy, he is so sweet. Which guy has ever made efforts to pick me up for a date? Which guy has got me chocolates and flowers on the first date? Which guy I know is passionate about designing a new app? He is too good to let go, come on Shona, go out and apologise instead of wasting time here in front of this mirror,' I criticised and inculpate my own behaviour.

I hastily walked back to our table in a spontaneous conscious state of mind; a bit confused, a bit nervous and carrying my depleted self confidence with an intention to apologise to Subrato, only to find that, Subrato wasn't present on our table. I looked around to find him, he was no where.

I stood there numb and quiet.

Subrato left.

I couldn't believe that he left leaving a note behind, 'sorry Shon-ali gotta go, it's an emergency,' I read it and stood there shat-tered, unshakable, yet shaken up by his note.

'OMG, I guess, he is offended because I didn't agree with his perception, I shouldn't have bring up my opinion with such a strong contextual relationship.' I said to myself. I stood there in silence, it took me more than a minute to accept that SUBRATO LEFT. I was so excited about meeting Subrato and on contrary the date ended miserably. Subrato didn't even bother to say me a good bye, he left with a note.

I stood there alone embarrassed and mortified as if every one around me was glaring at me, but actually everyone was busy in their own life and no one was bothered about the discombobu-late situation of my heart. I felt stabbed hard. It wasn't the first time a guy rejected me, I had to face rebuffs, refusals, betrayals, earlier too. I was already broken, Subrato only added to the mis-ery.

I collected myself and consoled myself, 'Shona you are stronger than this, it's ok, let's move on, be brave,' I picked up my bag and left.

As I headed to walk out, something inside me made me turn towards the bar section of the SEA ROCK lounge, I had never be-fore try my hand on alcohol in my entire life, but exasperation creeped into my veins and I felt a sudden urge to consume alco-hol (is this how the first time happens?)

●●●●●

I occupied a vinyl seat and leaned on the table in dejec-tion and agony. The bar tender approached me to take my order. I wanted to tell him that I am not a drinker, in fact I don't even know the names of drinks mentioned on the menu card, I wanted to tell him that the 'rejection from boys' is the main cul-prit which lead me here at the bar, but instead of explaining my heart and mind out, I plainly showed my index finger in the direction of a bottle to point out, 'gimme that one.'

'Are you sure ma'am?' the bar tender confirmed. He might have sensed that I'm not the boozing types. He was definitely an amateur in his job and his past years experience in the business might have given him an insight on deciding whether a patron is an alcoholic or a non alcoholic sober like me who is submerged in pain.

'Yeah, I'm sure. It is strong enough to knock off my brain and is tasty enough that I can gulp it down in a go,' I flaunt fake confidence to appear as if I wasn't a first time drinker. Honestly, I wasn't even sure if that was an alcohol or certain syrup used in cocktails, let alone taste.

'That's tequila ma'am,' he informed.

'Yeah, give me that,' I wasn't in the condition to interpret what was tequila. I was substantially away from the cause and effect of a particular alcohol, all I wanted was; to shut my brain and escape thoughts about Subrato or other guys who rejected me and betrayed me in past. Why do these guys have the power to make a girl's world shrink and revolve around them? Why a girl is so depended on a guy emotionally? Why do we girls seek security and stability in marriages? Are we girls designed like this or is it the society which has made such rules for us? I wanted to shut these ambivalent thought running in my mind sequentially.

The bar tender poured colourless liquid in tiny glass and served it to me along with salt and lemon.

I held the tiny glass between my thumb and index finger, paused for more than a minute wondering whether I should leave the drink, get up and get lost from the bar or I should stay and drink. I was in a dilemmatic situation; my body, mind and soul were not in synchronisation with each other. My soul passed on lucid signals to my mind that my body should give up the idea of consuming alcohol; whereas my mind wasn't in the disposition to accept my soul's instructions, so...................

I gulped in the liquid without giving it a second thought. It tasted yukk but it felt good.

I was chugging one after the other numerous shots, my head was queasy, but my body was feeling as light as air. I was feeling nauseous after a number of shots, but that delicate juncture of time passed away with the help of lemon and salt. It isn't that I support alcoholism or I'm an alcoholic but alcohol was serving my demand for the situation. People either get drunk to celebrate or to cry in pain, I was drinking out of rejection.

One after the other, patrons were flowing out of the bar, it was the time to shut, but I didn't want to leave, I just wanted to sit there and stay at the state of SILENCE. I didn't intend to be disturbed when suddenly a familiar face flashed in front of me, I squint my eyes to get a better glimpse, but the physiognomy appeared blurry.

'Shonali,' he said.

'Hey you sound like Vikram,' I uttered in a peculiar drunken idiolect.

'Shonali are you drunk?' I found him disquiet.

'Hey, you not only sound like Vikram, but you also look like Vikram,' I squint to obtained a better view of him as he stride closer to me, 'OMG you are Vikram, Vikram, do you know what happened?' I wasn't in a state of mind to interpret my feelings but I was happy to find Vikram around me, he felt like a bright glimmering ray of light among dark clouds. Even in the numb state, my mind was well aware about the positive effect of Vikram's presence in my life, his presence made me feel alive.

'Shonali I was so worried for you. Why was your phone switched off? Me and Risha tried your number a hundred times, why are you drunk? 'he fired me with questions. His discomfort was lucidly portrayed in his eyes and voice and behaviour.

'I'm not a kid, why were you worried for me?' I said to flaunt as if 'I don't care'. I turned around away from him in dismay. The bar tender, waiter and other staff were watching us as if they were watching a chilli hot series of famous sitcom. Vikram was embarrassed, but he managed to decipher my despondency and kept his calm.

'Look at your watch it's mid night and you are asking me why am I worried?' he held my hand and showed me the time on my wrist watch, he continued to speak, 'where is Subrato? Didn't he drop you home,' Apart from me, he was definitely aggravated by Subrato too, 'come let's go from here,' Vikram held my hand and dragged me to tug out.

'Subrato left me without even saying a good bye, lol, and you were expecting him to drop me home?' I looked deep into his eyes and expressed my melancholy, I released my hand from his grip and denied leaving the bar.

'Shonali, you are on your high, you are not in your senses, let's go from here,' he ignored my sob anecdote, I only wished to be heard by him. Instead of being empathic towards me, he agitatedly conveyed that he wish to avoid any further scene in the bar, so he emphasised on leaving the bar soon.

I ignored his urge to leave the bar and shoot my question, 'how did you know that I'm here?'

'I was in the last dialled of your contact list and the bar authority were generous enough to switch on your phone and call the first person in your contact list rather than calling cops,' he informed me, 'Shona let's just get the hell out of here,' his voice concerned and he sounded perturbed.

Vikram didn't wait for my denial this time, he simply held my hand and forced to drag me out.

I was walking as if the floor had banana peels all around, if Vikram wasn't handling me, I would have found my face against the ground. It was happening to me that a curtain was falling off the middle of the act leaving minutes in darkness and when I was back in my senses for minutes all I could witness was Vikram putting me in the rear seat of his car and driving fiercely in anger. The streets were smear through the window. I was drunk and high, my senses were out on a vacation. I was crying and laughing at a same point of time.

I twirled the knob to increase the volume of car's music system, my body waved in accordance with the cadence of the song played, 'you broke my heart baby,' and in every exactly next three seconds, I repeated, 'you broke my heart baby,' I sang out louder than ever, '- you broke my heart baby.'

'I want windows rolled down, I want to breathe in fresh air,' I demanded and resumed singing, 'you broke my heart, you took my smile and tore it apart, you broke my heart baby,' I unreasonably started laughing.

'Oh gosh Shona, relax, may be Subrato didn't lie to you, may be he really had to go, may be there was an emergency, he is a doctor, you must understand,' Vikram tried to calm me down as he parked the car.

'You broke my hearttttttttttt,' I ignored him as he supported me to get off the car, I sing even louder in the lobby, Vikram knew that he was about to face embarrassment but he managed somehow.

'You broke my heart baby,' I wrapped my arm across Vikram's broad shoulder and dragged my feet, stumbling on each step that I placed. He held me gently by my waist. His concern towards me was displayed in each small act that he did to protect me and preserve me.

'Shona just a few more minutes, we have almost reached home,'

Vikram expressed. He had to let me go for a moment while he pulled out the keys, he leaned me up against the wall while I began to slide down, he grabbed me by my waist before I hit the ground. I went limp and I relied on Vikram to be carried inside. Our eyes glued to each other, deep, intense and amorous. I had pain and misery in my eyes, which reflected onto his eyes.

'Where are we, this is not my home?' I swilled around and asked.

Vikram rested me on the couch and answered, 'this is my home.'

'Oh my God Vikram. Do you want to take advantage of a drunken girl? help help, help.' I squealed as he shut the door behind.

'Shut up Shona, you are under the influence of alcohol. Do you want to go home like this? What impact will you have on Risha when she will see you like this?' he yelled on me, he sounded logical. 'You can sleep in the bedroom, I'll sleep here on the couch,' he paused and looked deep into my eyes he kneel down, held my hand in his, his voice lowered, 'you are safe with me Shona, I'm here for you, don't worry,' he sounded genuine and concerned for me, 'for now please sit down until I get lemon water for you,' he expressed and stood up to leave.

'I'm not a doll Vikram,' I yanked his hand and didn't let him go, I made him sit, he came closer to me, I continued to speak, 'Shona sit here, Shona sit there, Shona stand like this, Shona walk like this, Shona talk like this, Shona behave like this, I'm not a doll Vikram,' I grabbed him by his collar, 'I'm not a doll, I have feelings, and feelings get hurt,' I looked deep into his eyes, my pain reflected onto his eyes. I gulped in my pain and restrained my tears to the utmost possibility.

'I'm sorry for yelling at you, I understand what you are feeling right now,' his voice low pitch, he held my hand with a tight grip, he came closer, and comforted me.

'Nobody understands me, nobody can love me, I'm not loveable,' I started crying as I released his collar and rested my head on his shoulder.

'No Shona you are amazing, you are loveable, you are beautiful,' he stroke my hair with utmost care and gentleness, his touch felt peace, if I were to write dictionary, I would have assigned 'peace' as a synonym for 'Vikram'.

'No, I'm boring, clingy and not worthy,' I said still crying like a baby.

'Shona you are a rare gem,' he comforted me like a baby.

'No, you are lying to comfort me, you don't mean what you say, nobody can love me, that's the truth,' I was still crying and couldn't resent my tears.

'I love you,' he confronted. Silence followed. I stopped crying and met my gaze with him, he peered at me without taking his eyes off. Our lips were mere an inch away, I was about to kiss him in that deplorable state but before I could kiss him, I puke out on the tavern floor, I bent down and I was still throwing out while Vikram was rubbing my back. 'Don't worry Shona, I'm here for you,' my hair covering my face had become soiled with my vomit. My clothes had become filthy and tattered. Vikram's living room was smelling of my foul vomit. I was still puking as Vikram held my hair behind my back and said, 'I can't see you like this Shona,' he continued to rub my back and I was still puking and coughing.

I finally stopped puking and Vikram made me sit down and grasp breath.

'Are you feeling better now?' He asked.

'Yeah,' I answered. Vomiting out made me feel better and helped me regain my consciousness, 'where's your washroom?' I asked.

I headed to washroom and cleaned myself, I changed into Vikram's oversized t-shirt and pyjamas.

When I returned, the living space was already cleared and lemon water was waiting for me on the table, 'are you feeling better?' Vikram inquired.

'Yeah,' I said and slept on the bed and Vikram covered me with a thin sheet.

●●●●●

#LOVETONIC 12 don't be judgemental or decisive on first date, may be he over talks out of excitement or may be he doesn't talks at all or talks on the minimum side out of nervousness. First date is less about the content and more about the behaviour. Observe his behaviour rather than focusing on the content of his talks. Grasp his perception and put up your perception clearly.

CHAPTER 13

When I woke up the next morning, my head was hammering, probably due to the hangover, 'Oh my god, so this is what hangover feels like?' when I got off the bed and it took me a moment to reconcile to my self that I was at Vikram's home. I couldn't recall much, but the blur images of the night before, slowly began to seep, like the morning mist, through my tired hangover brain.

I vaguely reminisced a few embarrassing events which ran in a sequence into my mind; the diegesis at the bar, my loud singing in the car, I was puking and crying like a wayward child. Among these faded images, the only thing which served as an evocative redolent for me was; Vikram's care and compassion towards me. His empathy, solicitousness and stoicism transformed me from the state of stormy and troubled to be calm and serene. I might have forgotten everything, but I didn't forget the way Vikram made me feel.

I swept out of the bed room and looked around to find Vikram, he was no where, probably he already left for the office. I was having a violent hangover and being an inexperienced drinker, I didn't exactly know the measures to be taken for subsiding a hangover. I felt lost in the strange apartment. I swivelled my eyes around Vikram's apartment and was amazed that his home wasn't a typical bachelor's dwelling, it was clean and neat, something which I hadn't expected. The need for order and organisation was apparent throughout. All the books on the shelves were arranged by the subject they covered, the CD's and records were also alphabetised and were arranged in a chronological order. The furniture were stark and the walls had an interesting pattern, each wall was occupied by a quote, the living room's wall said, 'quitters never win and winners never quit,' the kitchen's wall was interesting enough, it said, '3 C's cheese, chocolate, ~~coffee~~, chai.' A handmade Goddess Sarasvati clay idol sat in a corner. The wall parallel to the dining area, captivated me to my bewilderment, the entire wall was an aquarium which was a thriving den to umpteen in number but a sole species of fish, that was, gold fish. Tiny gold fishes swam across the huge tank to give an authentic marine appearance to Vikram's home.

I stopped wandering around the ambience and occupied the football themed bean bag, my spinning headache was getting worse and it was bothering me to the core, 'Oh god! Vikram, couldn't you wait for me to wake up, what was the urgency to leave for office?' My dependence on Vikram squealed out loud in pain assuming that I was alone in home, but within a fraction of second, Vikram's voice reached my ear tympanum, 'why are you yelling on the top of your voice?' Vikram emerged from the washroom, he was wrapped in a towel and droplets of water dribbled from his wet hair strands, his abs lucidly revealed the hard work and the time he devoted in the gym. His body was sculpted out of precision that of a super model. (Why is he wasting time in writing articles and editorials?) His smell of natural masculine musk was intense and was possibly a subject of generating obsession among girls.

'You didn't go office?' I asked illicit.

'How could have I left you alone? especially after what you were like last night,' I was feeling privileged to be under his tutelage, his each and every commiserating gesture towards me was drawing me closer to him.

He walked to the side drawer of his bed and drew out a small first aid kit box, he urgently tore off the silver foil packaging of the tablet, 'take this medicine,' he handed me the medicine, 'let me dress up, then I'll prepare some lemonade for you,' he shut the door.

I gulped in the aqua followed by swallowing medicine.

'You feeling better?' asked Vikram, he emerged out of his bedroom He dressed himself in a casual grey, black t-shirt and a blue denim. He brushed his hair and styled with gel, he appeared too sensuous to be despicable. There was a phase in my life, when I despised him the most, I was surely a maniac. The transition of that phase; from the point of despising Vikram to the point of depending on him for my emotional needs was crucially intense and amorous. Without my realisation, he grew to be an integral part of my life.

Vikram walked towards the kitchen. I followed him and occupied a chair on the dining table. He was busy squeezing juice out of a lemon into a tumbler and he poured in some cold water to it, along with adding seasoning.

'How are you feeling?' He repeated his question while he handed over the lemonade to me and initiated preparing chai for himself, the aroma arising from his masala chai indicated that he liked his tea mild and aromatic.

'Hmm, I'm feeling good,' I nodded as I sip in the lemonade. I was so embarrassed by my previous night's conduct, that I couldn't meet my gaze with him. I was struggling with appropriate words to establish a colloquy about previous night. *Should I start with 'did you sleep well last night?' come on Shona think of something better. Should I tell him that, 'I hope that the couch didn't give you an ache at the back.' Whatever Shona, come up with a better opening line. Should I directly bring up the three words, the big three words the 'I love you' three words, he uttered last night? Don't even dare to do that Shona, he might have just said them in a flow to bring you at ease so shut up and wait for him to start the conversation.* These brain racking and mind hacking inner conflicts were loading my nerves with trepidation and apprehension.

'Shona, you feeling better?' he asked me for the third time in a row, his expressions were rigid. He too was struggling with words to initiate the conversation about the previous night.

'Uhm Vikram,' I gathered all my courage to speak up, 'Vikram I'm sorry for my last night's behaviour,' I apologised. My gazed were fixated on the lemonade and I ran my finger counter clock wise along the rim of the glass tumbler.

'Are you sorry for me or for yourself?' he asked as he strained his tea and poured it in to a big black mug.

What was I sorry for? I didn't think of it before he mentioned. Was I sorry for drinking tequila shots one after the other and creating a brazen scene at the bar? Was I sorry for embarrassing Vikram ? Was I sorry because Vikram had to clean the puke for me? Was I sorry for myself that Subrato rejected me and left me without being courteous enough to say a good bye?

After giving it a brief thought, I came to a conclusion that, 'I'm sorry for you, I mean,' I stumble, 'I'm sorry to embarrass you and I'm sorry that I was a troublemaker for you, I'm sorry that you had to clear my puke.'

'If you are sorry for me, then please don't be sorry, I'm fine,' he said insouciant without a trace of smile on his face, it was strange to see Vikram without a grin, he seem to be a different person.

'Vikram, I know that you are furious and enraged because I was drunk last night, I embarrassed you and myself in the bar with my behaviour, but....' before I could camouflage my conduct with an explanation, Vikram carried his mug, occupied a chair next to mine and interrupted me, 'embarrassment is a part of everyone's journey Shona, each one of us have had an embarrassing moment, it's ok to be embarrassed. You are a human and your reaction was very natural, it's ok to be hurt. I appreciate your guts, you have never ever had a drink in your life time, you don't know a bit about alcohol and yet you did it, because you felt the need to do it. The positive side is, that you have learnt a lesson, you learnt that alcohol can make you behave miserable and I'm sure you don't want to repeat the act ever again,' he hearten my spirits, his voice was calm and serene. 'I'm not furious because you embarrassed yourself or you embarrassed me,' he placed his mug in an alignment with my lemonade glass.

'Then what is making you furious?' I asked unbend to clear my doubts. I sip in my lemonade.

'Before that, you answer my question, what made you drink?' he countered as he sip his hot beverage.

I shifted my gaze away from him and peered at my feet, I didn't had the courage to make an eye contact with him, 'Subrato rejected me,' I paused, 'he left a note and left me alone.' I answered unobtrusive, I sip in my lemonade and peered out the huge window to get a distant obfuscate view of the Arabian sea. Vikram's apartment was located at a distance from the beach front, the height and the locus, where he chose to reside, gave a fantastic Arabian sea view through the massive glass slider window.

'Shona he is doctor, may be he actually ran into an emergency, it could be a possibility na,' he answered logically, seeking my attention. The way he concluded his with na simply drove me crazy.

I left the chair to stand up, carried my tumbler, stride towards the massive window and occupied a place on the window sill. Speaking my heart out was easier while contemplating the sea rather then struggling to act furtive with Vikram, 'It wasn't only Subrato.' I continued, 'his handwritten note was a shadow cast of my past relations. I have been rejected and betrayed in past too. I am tired of rejections Vikram. My previous relations ended up in a not so good note.' I continued peering outside the massive window and spoke after a brief pause, 'May be I'm just not worth it Vikram, may be I'm not attractive enough, may be I don't have a good body, may be I don't know how to talk and what to talk, may be I don't have that calibre that charisma, I'm just good for nothing,' I counted out each hindrance which had become an usual part of my suppressive belief system.

'Shona,' he left his mug on the table, left his chair and walked towards me, he came closer to me and halt, I gathered strength and looked up at him, it was the first time in the entire morning, I met my gaze with his. He looked deep into my eye, his gaze was penetrating mine, the depth in his eyes, the warmth of his physicality blended into every cell of my body through his eye, 'Shona, your previous boyfriends didn't deserve you. None of them were worth you and you call your self worthless? This is the point one.' Vikram counted out on his index finger and lifted my spirit as he sat facing me on the window sill. I kept my tumbler aside.

'Going to point two,' he counted on his next finger and continued with a solution, 'about your body; you are not aware Shona, but girls of your age, hit gym at sharp 5 in the morning, kick their ass off until 8 in the morning and still don't get in to the shape that you already have.' He cupped my face with his palms, I could feel the warmth transferred via his hands onto my skin, he continued to make me feel awesome about myself, 'by chance, if you feel something is missing in you, one can always work for a solution rather than cribbing about it.' he said explicably, 'No one is perfect Shona.'

'Point number 3,' he continued with utmost clarity, 'about your attractiveness; you look more beautiful then any of those bimbos out there. Your eyes are naturally streak with kohl, your lips don't need a lipstick, your cheek bones don't need bronzer. If your were a McDonald's burger, the most popular burger wouldn't have been Mc Fillet o Fish or Mc Chicken, it would have been Mc Bengal tigress,' I couldn't help myself, but laughed out loud at his Mc Donald's joke, 'Oh my God Shonali, don't laugh out so loud, you don't know but the room lightens up with your smile and your laughter is dangerous enough to cause a lightening thunder. In fact when you walk on the road, you should walk with a warning sign board which should read 'WARNING: STARING AT ME FOR LONGER THAN A MINUTE CAN CAUSE YOU IRREGULAR HEART BEAT.' Vikram finished singing my ballyhoo and I was laughing whole heartedly. It felt as if he sprinkled his magic dust on me which instantly made me feel good about myself, he inflicted self love within me.

That was first time in the entire morning, I saw Vikram smiling, his smile was contagious and fervent. There was an authenticity in his smile, genuine and ardent.

As I discontinued laughing and Vikram picked up the colloquy, 'I don't believe it Shona, that you are questioning your own self and your own identity for a guy. I don't believe it that you are looking for your validation, recognition and consideration externally. If you look for your self outside, you will always end up being dishearten inside. Why is anybody's opinion so important to you? Why don't you create an opinion of your own self for your own self. Shona you have worked so hard on your self, on your principals, morals, ethics, your values, so, how come this one guy is making you question about your self? Do you seriously want to do this to YOURSELF? ask yourself Shona.'

'No, I don't want to do this to myself, but I followed love tonics for Subrato, I worked hard for him, I put in my efforts,' I justified myself.

'You worked hard for yourself not for him, you fool. LOVE TONICS are designed to extract the hidden persona inside you. It is about showing the polished side of you which is a better version of you. It's not about changing yourself, it's about upgrading yourself. It's all about being a girl with high integrity, high self esteem, high self respect and high self worth. It's about 'not chasing guys'. The true essence of LOVE TONICS is about letting a guy notice a girl's worth. If the guy doesn't notices your worth, it simply means that, he is not worth you. LOVE TONICS doesn't assure you a successful relationship, but it definitely assures you a better you. The day you start investing your time, energy, money and love on to your own self the world will follow you.'

'It sounds simple but it's not easy,' I countered stubborn.

'It is easy Shona. Well, rejection and non adaptability is one and the same thing. It is time to be adaptable Shonali. There is a lot you can do with yourself, like; pick up your hobby and polish your skill, find your purpose of life, follow your passion, work on overcoming your fear,' he said to transform me, 'come on choose any one of them,' he asked. I was aware that there are four types of speaker, one is informational speaker, this category of speaker speaks to share his piece of information. Second is motivational speaker, this category of speaker will influence you with his stories but the influence doesn't lasts long. Third category of speaker in an inspirational speaker, who inspires you to get up instantly and take an action to chase your dream and the fourth type of speaker is transformational speaker, who blends in with your soul and transforms your life. Vikram was the category four.

I looked up at him and chose, 'over coming my fear.'

'Great, close your eyes,' he commanded.

'What?' I asked lost.

'Close your eyes,' he repeated and ran his hand over my eyes to close them.

'What's your fear? Think about your fear,' he leaned in closer and whispered in my ears.

'The fear of stage,' I uttered. 'I remember the instance when I was in school, I collapsed on the stage during a poetry recitation competition. With passing time, I thought I have overcome my fear, but a similar incident repeated itself when I was in college when I was suppose to play sitar for a jugalbandi concert at the college fest, but no sooner did the curtains were raised than I faced the crowd I was what are you feeling......... ' my eyes were still shut and I could express my feelings to him unobstructed.

'You play sitar,' he sounded impressed, 'answer while your eyes are closed, don't open your eyes,' he commanded. My eyes were closed yet I could sense Vikram's contemplating me.

'Yeah. Baba taught me to play sitar,' I reminisced. It was a bit awkward to speak while my eyes were closed, the rhythm of my voice was in a synchronisation with Vikram's breath. I expressed my memories, 'Vikram, while I play sitar, time reverses itself and hauls me back to the halcyon moment when I was a ten year old girl. I recall every single evening when I used to wait for baba to return home, so that he could teach me to play sitar. My baba was a reputable music teacher,' my voice tranquil, Vikram heard me with stillness. There was an awkward peace present in that moment which carried my past and present both. I could feel Vikram's heart beat with every word that I said.

When I opened my eyes, Vikram stood still, he was staring at me, staring and staring, his mouth hanged in amazement. He was staring at me as if he was reading me, I looked at him blankly and for once he stopped staring at me, he looked away from me at a distance, contemplating something.

'Shona,' he uttered. I loved the way he said my name, he looked at me.

'hmm,' I responded.

'Take up a challenge,' he offered his hand, 'I Vikram Khanna, challenge you Shonali Sen, to work on yourself and take a step ahead towards getting over your fear and free yourself from Glossophobia.' I looked at his hand and shifted my gaze to peer his expectant eyes, 'The day you get over your fear, you will realise the real essence of true love, because you will fall in love with yourself. Studies reveals that fear of public speaking is basically a fear of criticism and a fear of rejections. *#LOVETONIC 13 get over your fear: identify your fear and get over it, the day you get over your fear, you will fall in love with your self, self love is more important that any other love. You will realise the need and importance of being adaptable. You will move out of your comfort zone and walk a step towards your higher self.*

I gave a brief thought, I recalled the insulting, ignominious situation which I faced in past due to my fear. Despite of being a highly reputable music teacher's daughter, I failed to play a simple note on sitar, I have never forgiven myself for bringing that ignominy to my father. I didn't talk about it with Baba, because I crashed Baba's expectations. Though Baba never expressed his dismay, but it was understood that Baba gave up his expectations regarding my stage performance. Baba wanted me to replace him in the musical event which was held every year in Kolkata, but the callous incident made it very clear that he was seeking right things from wrong person.

'I can't do this, I know myself and I can't. I mean.....' I uttered spontaneously.

Vikram appeared rebuffed, 'if you can't do this, then simply move on to the next guy and reach out your hand for what you exactly want, 'YOUR BORING SECURITY AND STABILTY' but remember that you are looking for security and stability under the influence of your mother and society, may be this isn't exactly what you want,' he said provocative. Vikram leaned into me, his lips were mere an inch away from mine, our eyes glued to each other, each nerve in my body was responding to his heart beat, we looked into each other's eyes, he wanted to say something but his lips denied to speak, I paid my attention to heed the unsaid. Did he wanted to kiss me or it was me who wanted to be kissed by him. The intense air between us was as confused as we were. At the same point of time, my phone bleeped to indicate a call received.

'My phone,' I withdraw myself from his aura and heaved. There was some awkwardness running between us, something which I wanted I didn't wanted but I was craving for. This ambivalent feeling was driving me crazy.

'It's out there,' Vikram pointed towards the side table of his bed, 'I put it on chargin, the batteries were dead,' he acknowledged me.

'That's so thoughtful of you,' I said as I walked towards his bedroom and reached for my phone to take the call.

'That must be Risha, she must be worried about me,' I muttered as I picked up my phone.

'Naah, I informed her about your whereabouts,' he said. He stood in an akimbo leaning on the door.

The call was disconnected before I could reach it, I saw the notification to find that the call was from Subrato.

Vikram read my numb expressions, 'who's that,' he asked.

'Subrato,' I said in one breath. I clicked to check call logs, it read, 'OMG, 73 missed calls from Subrato.' Let me check texts, 'aww he says, I'm so sorry Shonali but I had an emergency, there was a road accident case, I had to run leaving you behind, I tried your phone umpteen number of times as soon as I got free from the operation theatre, but I guess you are so offended that you switched off your phone, just talk to me once.'

I looked up at Vikram, seeking his response, he shrugged indifferent and said, 'reply that it's ok, tell him that I totally understand, I left my phone at a friend's place last night and I'm not at all offended.'

I typed and as soon as I sent the text, arrived his reply, 'Talk to me once please, I wanna listen your voice.' I readout the text for Vikram, waiting for next reply.

Vikram commanded, 'tell him, I can't talk right now, I'm in middle of some thing important, I'm sorry.'

'Let's meet up today, I'll pick you from office or home, or where ever you say, please give me a chance,' Subrato replied.

'Subrato sounds genuine Shona,' said Vikram.

'What do I reply,' I asked Vikram.

'#LOVETONIC 14 neither accept an offer immediately nor decline it at once, take time to reply even if you know the response in your mind. If you accept it once you will sound desperate and if you decline or reject promptly, you will sound ungrateful,' explained Vikram, 'So tell him that I'll let you know as soon as I get free,'

I obeyed him

'Come let's have breakfast,' Vikram invited.

●●●●●

I occupied a seat on dining table adjacent to the wall which had a fish tank built in it. My mind was still wandering over Subrato's call, while Vikram was busy preparing a concoct with utmost diligence. The way he handled the pan with his left hand and he held the ladle with the right one clearly indicated that he was an amateur in cooking skills, 'so you cook?' I asked impressed.

'Yeah, I'm kinda multi talented,' he winked, 'I have travelled world and have learnt a lot from my experiences, I'm living in a suitcase ever since I was in grade eight.

'What are you cooking?' I asked when familiar aroma hit my

nostrils.

'Luchi and cholar dal,' he smiled as he announced the Bengali delicacy.

'You cook Bengali food!!!! More over do you like Bengali food?' I asked in bewilderment.

'Who told you that I don't like Bengali food? Of course I love Bengali cuisine, it will interest you to know that my mom was a Bengali,' he beamed with the thought of his mom.

Oh, so he has Bengali genes running in his veins, interesting!!!

Vikram continued after a pause, 'I thought why not, do something Bengali special for this beautiful Bengali girl,' his enunciation was as clear as a Bengali descendant. *RED ALERT: Is he trying to flirt? Come on he called me beautiful, that's how guys start flirting.* 'My mom cooked delicious cholar dal, God I miss her so much,' he eulogized while he served the cholar dal in a bowl and reached refrigerator to draw out the pickle jar.

'I am sorry about your mom,' I offered my condolences to him.

'Its ok,' he concealed his emptiness behind the feigned grin, he continued with an attempt to flip the melancholic leitmotif, 'by the way reminiscing cataclysmic memories or talking sad stuff isn't allowed on dining table, consequently, there are chances that we may experience bad sex life for next five years,' he came up with this illicit theory all of a sudden with facetious remarks, 'and I definitely don't want a bad sex life for myself,' he concluded.

'What????? Who came up with this stupid theory about bad sex life?' I asked feeling curious and amused at a same point of time.

'Vikram Khanna,' he proudly announced his name and we broke into a laughter in an unison over his whimsical sense of humour. Vikram placed the hot bowl of cholar and a plate filled with luchi along with pickle. The food looked so good that I couldn't wait any further.

I dipped a piece of luchi in hot cholar and masticated the concoct. I asked Vikram, 'what's your obsession with gold fish, I mean why don't you have any other species of fishes in your fish tank?'

Vikram peered at the fish tank which aligned the dining table, he spots a small gold fish and amiably alludes to the fish, 'they are my Goldilocks,' his eyes twinkled as they followed the small gold fishes as they swam across the tank. He said as he aided some pickle on to his luchi.

'Goldilock?' I inquired to synchronize with his strange deportment.

'Yeah, Goldilock, that was my gold fish's name. Did I mention you that I pet a gold fish when I was ten years old,' he confronted.

'No, you didn't,' I nodded.

The food tasted as good as it appeared, I cleared the dining table and placed empty dishes in the sink. Vikram didn't move from his seat. I poured water for us in two glasses and returned to dining table, I occupied a seat next to Vikram as he continued with his anecdote, 'I loved Goldilock so much that I broke up with my first girlfriend for her,' he conveyed his displeasure.

'You had a girlfriend when you were ten years old???' I asked amazed.

'She wasn't important but Goldilock was,' he played his finger on the rim of the glass as he expanded, 'My girlfriend had a kitty named Calibre. Despite of hundred warnings, my girlfriend always tagged along calibre to my home. One eve while me and my girlfriend were busy solving math equations, that feline Calibre, ate my Goldilock,' he paused with dismay, 'so I broke up with my girlfriend,' he said, he stopped running his finger over the rim of the glass and placed it aside.

He did most of the talking in the entire morning *and on contrary we girls are notorious for being talkative and loquacious.*

'That's insanely too much to do for just a fish,' my eyebrows raised in surprise, 'some one like Vikram Khanna could break up with girl friend for a pet fish,' I mocked as I sipped in some water.

'Goldilock wasn't just a fish, she was my family after mom and dad died in the car accident,' he admitted.

His revelations made me numb for a second or two, I could not gulp in the aqua, neither could I throw it out, I couldn't grasp the lugubrious fact that he lost his both parents at the age of ten and found himself orphan. Life had been atrociously cruel on him, I couldn't believe that an ebullient person like Vikram had been through such a calamitous childhood.

I was lost in ideating Vikram's childhood without his parents. 'Shonali' he alluded, while I was still in an oblivious state. I looked up at Vikram's despondent eyes as he continued to speak, 'each death that I witnessed, split me into two parts; one part was, what I was and other was, what I could have been. It lead me in an impossible situation with no solution. I dreamed about my parents every night for nearly until I was a teen, I still do dream of them occasionally. I dream playing carom board with mom and dad in our old home,' his lips curved up to a smile oblivious, 'the dreams are so real that it's difficult for me to differentiate between virtual and real. At times, in my dreams, I am playing hide and seek with mom,' he smirks, his face lightens up as he mentioned his mom, 'mom hides in a corner behind the staircase and I couldn't find her, suddenly the fear creeps in my mind, that mom is hiding away at such a distance where I'm unable to reach her. I am unable to breathe after that moment, I fall in a state of sleep paralysis, I'm bathed in sweat, stuck between reality of my life and hallucination of my dream, I wake up after a brief struggle of asphyxia, a big silence, a long pause and it is all over when I open my eyes,' his arched smirk metamorphosed into dejected grim. His forehead formed small pears of sweat dribbling off his cheek.

'Have water Vikram,' I offered him some water as he resumed to delineate his anecdote, 'My parents married against their respective parent's will. My maternal grandparents didn't at all attend my parents funeral, they claimed that my mom died for them on the day she married my dad. Situations with my paternal grandparents too were more or less similar, but my daadi and my uncle were generous enough to accept me, while the rest of the world abandoned me.'

I said nothing but peered at him, his voice was so low that he was barely audible, I leaned closer to him so that he was clearly audible to me.

'I moved in with my daadi and uncle, they were kind and humble, they tried to fill in the dent in my life which was caused by my parent's death. Daadi was taking care of my needs; both emotional needs as well as material needs.'

Tear rolled off my eyes. I placed my hand over his, oblivious to my dilemma, whether I was trying to console him or was seeking solace for myself. I said nothing but looked at him for a brief span of time while he shifted his gaze on mine, 'I'm sorry to make you cry,' he said.

'Are you fine?' I asked.

'I'm fine,' he said concealing his emptiness behind the feigned grin.

I said with an attempt to flip the melancholic leitmotif, 'by the way reminiscing cataclysmic memories or talking sad stuff isn't allowed on dining table, consequently, the diners will experience bad sex life for next five years,' I wiped my tears and repeated his illicit theory all of a sudden with facetious remarks, 'and I know that you definitely don't want a bad sex life for yourself.'

'Who came up with this stupid theory?' He half smiled with his wet eyes and asked. The dialogues were same the participants them had shifted a flip.

'Vikram Khanna,' I proudly announced his name and we broke into a laughter in an unison.

●●●●●

#LOVETONIC 13 get over your fear: identify your fear and get over it, the day you get over your fear, you will fall in love with your self, self love is more important that any other love. You will realise the need and importance of being adaptable. You will move out of your comfort zone and walk a step towards your higher self.

#LOVETONIC 14 neither accept an offer immediately nor decline it at once, take time to reply even if you know the response in your mind. If you accept it once you will sound desperate and if you decline or reject promptly, you will sound ungrateful,' explained Vikram, 'So tell him that I'll let you know as soon as I get free,'

CHAPTER 14

'Shona di, did you find it here?' asked Risha, I stood on the top of the step stool, my head in one of the upper storage cabinet, moving the paraphernalia down onto the counter.

'No Risha, it's not here too,' I replied dejected as I descended the step stool and landed on the ground. My hair were tied up into a messy bun, my nostrils had underwent a wide range of mould odour which is usually caused due to microbial volatile organic compounds, my lungs were filled with dust, I managed to escape a dozen of spider webs and dust webs, it was two in the noon and I was still hanging around in my pyjamas without bathing myself right from the time I woke up at six in the morning. If at all, my mom was cognizant with my anomalous behaviour, she would have either propelled me in to a tub full of water or she would have emptied a bucket full of water on me. I prefer the later more than former though.

'May be we kept it in Nirmala aunty's garage, we should check out there,' Risha lead a trail of clue as she coughed due to dust which she inhaled in the process of our search quest.

'No, we kept it in Sharma uncle's garage after Diwali Puja,' I recalled last diwali puja and denied following Risha's clue.

'No, we kept it in Nirmala Aunty's garage,' Risha argued confidently.

'Okay, you go and check Sharma aunty's garage and I'll check Nirmala uncle's garage,' I was so tired and messed up with my eight hours nonstop search quest that I toggled with names.

'Shona di calm down,' Risha suggested she offered me a thin neck bottle filled with water.

'I mean you go and check Sharma uncle's garage and I'll check Nirmala aunty's garage,' I rectified myself as I gulp in the aqua.

'Shona di, I'm tired, even you are messed up, let's take a break for now and resume our search hunt post lunch,' Risha suggested.

'No way, we are searching for it right now,' I kept the bottle aside and said adamantly.

After failing the frantic scan of Sharma Uncle's garage, Risha rushed towards me, she was panting and gasping for breath in order to speak, she bent down and held her knees for support, 'Shona di,' she said as she inhaled some oxygen.

'Did you find it?' I asked.

'Mice,' Risha uttered another word as she heaved another breath.

'Don't tell me that you came running to me because you saw a mice,' I laid my guess work.

'No, I mean yes,' she babbled, ' I mean, yes when I saw a mice, I recalled that I wrapped your SITAR in a bubble wrap and kept it beneath your bed in your room to keep it out of the reach of mice and other rodents, we are unneccarily searching for it else where,' she confronted while she was still panting.

'OMG Risha, couldn't you recall this earlier.' I heaved a sigh of relief, so did she.

●●●●●

'I need a shower,' Risha picked up her towel and left me alone with my sitar.

I unwrapped my most valuable belonging, 'my priceless SITAR'. I held it in my hand as if I was holding my childhood. I laid my amorous eyes on it and peered at it wholeheartedly. I felt fulfilled and complete, nothing on earth gave me the happiness and peace equivalent to my sitar. It was undeniably extortionate belonging to me because it was my Baba's sitar, I had my emotions and Baba's blessing attached to it. I wondered in dismay that I ceased to play it and I couldn't believe myself that I discontinued the only task which gave me immense pleasure and happiness.

I tuned and adjusted the strings to avail the perfect rhythm and placed it in a position parallel to myself and picked up an intricate melody on sitar. I closed my eyes and I struck each string with adherence and devotion. Each tone of the theme transpired me to an utter state of peace. I was lost, immersed and engrossed into music, I was loving to play sitar after such a long time.

While I was playing sitar, all in had in my mind was Vikram. His words echoed in my ears, those three words I LOVE YOU, he confronted lucid and clear on the other night when I was drunk. I wasn't in my senses but Vikram was sober and was in a state of complete sense, but I had a pinch of doubt that he might have uttered those three special words to comfort me. Whether he really mean those words or he uttered them in a flow, whether he really did love me or they were just words for him? I needed an answer to my questions.

When I opened my eyes after a long span of time, I found Risha sitting adjacent to the wall, facing me, her eyes closed and she as well was immersed in the music.

'When did you come back, your usual showers aren't so short,' I commented to haul Risha back into reality from her subjective state of mind.

'Your sitar melodies are more refreshing and stress relieving then shower,' she said astonished. 'Shona di, your melodies pay off for all the hard work we did in the search quest,' she commented, 'you play exactly like baba.'

'I learned from him after all,' I smirked with pride. I zipped my sitar in its bag carefully and placed it aside.

I walked to the kitchen to prepare some coffee for us. The aroma of coffee hitting my nostrils was the perfect and only thing I needed after the serene sitar session.

'But Shona di, I don't understand your sudden urge to play sitar,' Risha's voice emerged from the room. She was too lazy to leave her cosy place in the room.

'Vikram is the reason,' I answered in higher note, so that my voice from the kitchen reached to her in the room.

'Vikram told you to play sitar???????' Risha left her cosy place and came running to the kitchen, she sounded amazed and bewildered.

'No you fool,' I poured coffee for us in our respective gratitude mugs, carried the mugs and walked back to the room, she followed me intrigued, I offered a mug filled with coffee to Risha, 'he told me that,' I paused to sip in some coffee, mimicked Vikram's voice and repeated his words, 'Shona, rather than struggling and wasting time behind FINDING the person who makes you happy, instead, BE that person who makes you happy.' I smiled and continued, 'Risha, his love tonics are not only love tonics; his tonics are making me love myself, his love tonics are driving me closer to my own self, his love tonics are helping me in finding myself, I'm loving the brand new me.' I said when I finished necking down my coffee.

'I too love the brand new you, I'm so happy to see you happy,' Risha said as she slurp her coffee.

I walked back to the kitchen with empty mugs and came rushing back to Risha without placing them in the sink, I realised that it was the perfect time to talk to Risha about the girl in Vikram's life, 'Risha you and Vikram have become good friends right?' I fenced out the topic in a hope to seek revelation from her.

'Yeah,' she uttered casually unware about my intentions.

'The other day when you came to the office, uhm' I babbled, 'I heard you and Vikram were talking about a girl, may be his love of life or something like that,' I gathered courage and asked straight, 'Vikram sounded serious about that girl, is she someone special?' I paused, 'who's that girl?' I bit my lower lips out of curiosity and was waiting impatiently for a reply from Risha.

'Oh!!! that girl,' uttered Risha to intrigue me, 'Shona di, eavesdropping is a bad habit.'

'Don't take me wrong, I wasn't eavesdropping, I happened to pass from there and heard your conversation unintentionally. I'm just asking you out of my curiosity,' I tried to appear unmoved and casual.

'Don't mind , but like #LOVETONIC, even friendship come with certain rules and regulations. I don't want to break any rule by sharing Vikram's secrets with you, hope you don't mind and hope you understand,' said Risha.

'I understand,' I faked an absorbing countenance.

'By the way, you sound affected by the other girl,' inquired Risha to tease me.

'No, not at all, I'm not at all affected,' I feigned.

'How is it going with Subrato?' Risha asked to change the topic.

'Subrato is apologetic about leaving me at the cafe, he had an emergency case to be attended, he wants me to give him another chance,' I said.

'And what do you want?' she asked.

'I don't know, I'm not sure about Subrato,' I answered vaguely.

'I think you should give him a chance Shona di,' suggested Risha, ' he fulfils almost all the criteria in your check list, he sounds promising and genuine.'

My phone bleeped to indicate a text received from office and I got a valid reason to escape from Risha and her sagacious advise.

I excused myself and dressed up in my regular fabindia kurta which I paired it with denim.

'I gotta go office, I'm late, bye Risha,' I said and left her vicinity.

●●●●●

When I reached office, except Vikram and Deepika, the entire team was present in the conference room with. Collaboration with MODE DE VIE was a great opportunity, not only for Kartik, but for every member in the team. They had a huge fan base and the news of it collaboration with ADD IT TUDE was a wild fire among the loyal fans, readers were expecting us to reach a higher bench mark in terms of content and context.

I occupied my regular spot beside Kartik at the conference room. Kartik gazed at his wrist watch and commented, 'these love birds are taking too long to arrive for the meeting.'

'Love birds?' I uttered in a shock, 'who are the love birds?'

'Who else, Vikram and Deepika,' uttered Kartik, fumes burst out of my nose the moment I heard the two names together, my palms clenched to form a fist and I wanted to bang the table with my rigidly clenched fist, but I managed to maintain my composure. *So Deepika is the one..... I should have guessed it earlier.* I unscrew the packaged water and gulped in to calm myself down. I wasn't able to interpret my deportment. *Was I angry because that girl was Deepika (I shared not a balanced equation with Deepika) or would I have been equally angry with any other girl who replaced Deepika in Vikram's life. Was I angry or was I jealous???? These question marks were big puzzles to be solved by me.*

Amrita jumped in the conversation and said, 'You look shocked Shonali, don't you know what's cooking between them? The entire office knows their story,' she enlightened with extra lemon and spice to the leitmotif of gossip.

'But Deepika is engaged, she has a fiancé waiting for her back in her home town, how can she be in a relationship with Vikram ?' I questioned the existence of Vikram's relationship with Deepika.

'Ping, which bubble are you living in?' Kartik mocked at me. He drew out his phone, opened his Instagram app and displayed a few images to me, 'Well Check this,' he showed me images of the twosome hanging out at these beachfront with their hands in the back pockets of each other's jeans. Another image displayed their endearment by sharing an ice-cream from a single cone. Next image showed the fun time they spent while watching a movie. I recalled that Vikram clarified to me that Deepika was only a casual fling for him, but none of the images displayed casualness. The images clearly indicated that Vikram didn't love me, he might have uttered those three important words in order to comfort me.

'Is this Deepika's Instagram?' I inquired, 'I have stalked Vikram's Instagram a couple of times,' I admitted, 'but none of these images are present in his Instagram account. These images are displayed only on Deepika's Instagram account,' without realising I tangled myself in an argument regarding Vikram and Deepika's relationship status, my heart was not willing to accept that duo were having an affair.

'May be Vikram wants to be secretive about their relationship and on contrary Deepika wants to flaunt their relationship,' Kartik supported the images with his suppositions and assumptions.

'Look there they are, let's pretend as if we don't know anything about them,' said Amrita while she gazed at the see through glass, she saw Vikram and Deepika arriving towards the conference room.

I shifted my gaze in their direction as they stepped in the conference room together, they occupied a seat next to each other and looked at each other with eyes filled with amour. I felt as if Vikram had betrayed me, even though he hadn't. We were just friends and Vikram had the liberty to date any one. Technically, even I was dating Subrato. Subrato apologised for leaving me alone at the cafe and he asked me out for another date, so basically Subrato and me were still on, but Vikram and Deepika were bothering my peace in any case.

I shifted my gaze away from the couple, 'Well today's agenda for team meet is,' Kartik initiated the meet, 'discussing the planning of the launch event party and agreement signing of ADD IT TUDE with MODE DE VIE '

'Woohoo!!!!' exclaimed Vikram, he smirked at me and I ignored. The entire team was cheering except for me, I wasn't comfortable with the fact that Vikram was having a serious scene with Deepika.

'The launch party is on Monday.' Informed Kartik. 'Vikram and Deepika, I want to assign an important task to you two,' Kartik called their names together. The two were blushing like a newly wedded couple and I disliked that their names were being called out together. I couldn't bear it any more, I needed some fresh air, so I excused my self pretending to receive a fake call, 'I'll have to take this call,' I said and left the conference room in a ziff.

•••••

I stepped out of office and descended downstairs to avail some fresh air. I strolled along the belt of Ashoka tress which fenced the compound of the edifice. While I was on my promenade, busy disentangling my ambiguous eventualities of life, I noticed a familiar frame stood at the distance on the other side of the road. I perambulated closer to find that, the familiar human frame was Subrato, he stood at the exactly same spot, from where he picked me up on the previous evening. I was flabbergasted by his effort. For a moment, series of thoughts ran into my mind; I looked at my self, I was a perfect mismatch in a fabindia kurta which I paired with denim. I definitely didn't want Subrato to see in that outfit.

'Hi,' he waved his hand from a distance, he leaned casually on the bonnet of his car.

I kept my concerns aside and cautiously crossed the road to reach him. He stood tall and erect dressed in a beige pants and an olive green t-shirt. His facial countenance appeared sanguine but his body squirmed out of anxiety and nervousness.

'Indo-western outfit suits on you Shonali,' he initiated a conversation.

'Thank you,' I said as I was waiting for him to disclose the reason of his unexpected appearance at my office edifice.

'I'm sorry to drop off by your office like this, neither I intend to disturb you nor do I want to stalk you outside your office,' he expressed his intentions. 'I'm not such a guy who stalks a girl, but when it comes to you, I can't help myself, I become restless. I dropped so many texts and tried calling you umpteen number of times , but you didn't seem to reply, so I thought of waiting here for you,' he explicably clarified his presence in the vicinity of my office.

'I'm so sorry Subrato, I checked your texts, but I was too busy to reply,' I defended.

'Shona, I'm really sorry for leaving you at the cafe with a note. Trust me, if it weren't an emergency accident case, I would have never left you like that,' he sounded desperate.

'I understand Subrato and I told you that it's ok. I'm not offended, you don't need to be sorry. I'm glad that you are such high on your professional ethics,' I said.

He said nothing but smiled, he appeared relieved, he stared at me for longer than a minute.

'What?' I half giggled, 'why are you staring at me like this?'

'I'm wondering that how can a girl be so understanding, usually girls get mad on boys on such behaviour, but you are different Shonali, you are easy to be with.'

'Thanks,' I said. I recalled *#LOVETONIC 14 if you are yearning for a commitment from a guy in your relationship, then, comes the most crucial and important think to do; BE A GIRL WHO IS EASY TO BE WITH. Boys find it hard to fall in a committed relationship with a girl who is a difficult person to be with, who is constantly trying to change him, constantly nagging him for petty things, constantly trying to curb his freedom to breathe and his space to dwell. A girl can only be easy to be with when, sheer is independent and enough for her own self. In order to keep a guy happy, first learn to be happy with your own self, be enough for your own self.*

'Shonali,' he called out, 'if you really aren't mad at me, can we please go out for dinner tonight,'

'Umm, Subrato..'

'Please don't keep me waiting for your reply, your silence with long impedes make me go crazy,' he said.

I said nothing but recalled the #LOVETONIC 13, I peered at him with dilemmas in my mind and tangled myself into a conflict between my heart and my mind;

My mind: Shona, you shouldn't accept a date immediately nor should you decline it at once.

My heart: Forget accepting and declining a date, do you really wish to go out with Subrato? all you have in your thoughts is Vikram.

My mind: Vikram is dating Deepika. Accept the dinner date with Subrato, he is seeking a chance to develop a bond with you.

My heart: say a no Shonali, don't do things which you don't feel like doing, don't go out with him.

I deceived my heart and made up my mind, I was about to say a NO , but Subrato spoke before I could decline, 'Shonali,' Subrato looked into my eyes and said, 'I really like you and I want to spend some time with you, I want to know more about you. I have been thinking of you ever since I have met you,' he paused, 'Come with me for dinner tonight and then you can decide whether you wish to see me further. If you don't want to meet me after tonight, it'll be totally your decision, I will never trouble you or try to influence your decision, but please give me a chance,' he tried to convince me.

'Uhm, Subrato,' I uttered, suddenly my eyes fell on Vikram and Deepika, they made an exit from the office edifice, they slipped into Vikram's car and swiftly drove off. Watching them together hand in hand was a major turn off for me, my stomach clenched drifting blood apart from my navel, my anger served as a fuel and I soon turned around to face Subrato, 'Yes,' I uttered spontaneous, 'yes, let's meet up for dinner tonight,' I confirmed the dinner date with Subrato.

Subrato's face illuminated with happiness, 'yes!!!!!' he exclaimed as if he cleared a clash of clans saga. 'I'll pick you from home,' he said. 'Thank you Shonali, you made my day,' he didn't need words to express his happiness, his facial countenance did the job.

'I'll get back to work, bye,' I said and turned around to leave his vicinity.

'Shonali,' he alluded.

'hmm,' I turned around to meet my gaze with his.

'Can't wait to see you tonight,' he said.

I said nothing but faked an empty smile, left his vicinity and walked my way back into the office.

#LOVETONIC 14 if you are yearning for a commitment from a guy in your relationship, then, comes the most crucial and important think to do; BE A GIRL WHO IS EASY TO BE WITH. Boys find it hard to fall in a committed relationship with a girl who is a difficult person to be with, who is constantly trying to change him, constantly nagging him for petty things, constantly trying to curb his freedom to breathe and his space to dwell. A girl can only be easy to be with when, sheer is independent and enough for her own self. In order to keep a guy happy, first learn to be happy with your own self, be enough for your own self.

CHAPTER 15

Subrato picked me from the entrance of my lane, I could have called him to drive his car inside the lane but it was too early to disclose my exact locus of residence. I retrospect the austerity in Vikram's voice while he instructed to me the #LOVETONIC 15 don't reveal your residential address at an initial stage, even if the guy is coming over to pick you up or drop you off.

I accoutred myself in a teal wrap dress which accentuated my sylphlike waist. I adorned myself with a diaphanous bracelet on left wrist, onto its corner, a lock and key charm playfully hanged. I streaked my eyes with kohl, I applied a light shade of pink water lip gloss and tied my bangs into a high and neat pony tail. I looked up at the mirror and it casted an image of a svelte and sophisticated girl.

Subrato appeared more scrumptious than the previous coffee date, he wore a sky blue pinstriped formal shirt and paired it with a beige shade of chino pants. His musk was strong, sensuous and masculine, his hair were gelled generously and styled appropriately.

Subrato handed his car keys to a personnel in livery for valet parking and we walked across the porch inside a huge gate which lead us to *'FISHING BOAT authentic Bengali cuisine' I was extremely delighted to* read the huge L.E.D sign board in bold italics.

I was flabbergasted by the restaurant's ambience. The under-water or the submarine themed restaurant was swivelled by large fish tanks concealing the three corresponding walls. Ump-teen species of aquatic fauna and flora which dwelled there, were bringing the place to life, inflicting a palpable submarine effect and a splendid under water dining experience. Tables and chairs were styled in the shapes of waves and other aqua marine attractions. Subrato had arranged reservation for one such table behind the mini wine cellar which stood in a corner, adjacent to a fish tank which was infiltrated with copious number of poly-chromatic coloured small fishes. We sat in such a position align-ing the fish tank, that it appeared like a psychedelic abstract painting on our background. I was very excited with the idea of the theme of dining in an underwater ambience.

'I must tell you, you have an amazing choice when it comes to selecting restaurants,' I complimented Subrato as he pulled out a chair for me.

'You can never doubt my choice,' he gestured flirt.... pointing out to me.

I said nothing but blushed.

A waiter adorned in an outfit analogous to a character from the movie *Pirates of Caribbean* arrived with sparkling water and menu cards, he placed the menu on the table before us and left our vicinity.

I lift the menu and touted my favourite mouth watering delica-cies on eight page booklet, 'sorshe illish, macher jhol.' I read in my mind.

'Shonali,' Subrato beamed.

'hmm,' I kept the menu aside and heeded him.

'The other evening when we met, I umm,' he babbled out of nervousness.

'Tell me,' I encouraged him to speak.

'The other evening, whatever little time I spent with you,' he paused, I gazed him, 'was beautiful,' he smirked and continued, 'I loved the way you put up your point on technology and how mobile phones and applications have affected our lives, I appreciate your point of view. I appreciate your logical and strong perception.'

'I'm glad you abide with me,' I said as a smile danced on the corner of my lips.

While Subrato was busy placing his order I contemplated the fish tank adjacent to our table and my gaze shifted at a small gold fish, my face gleamed with a radiant smile, I soon retrospect Vikram's goldilock and the entire tale behind his goldilock.

'Shonali,' Subrato's voice transported me back to the restaurant from Vikram's home.

'Yeah,' I answered lost.

'You look more beautiful when you blush and smile like this,' he complimented me. I didn't even realise that I was blushing while Vikram's thought was running in my mind.

'Thank you,' I said while I poured some water for us in our glasses.

'Place your order please,' requested Subrato.

'Hello, good evening,' I looked up at waiter and greeted him, 'a sorshe illish will do fine for me,' I placed my orders and smiled profusely. #LOVETONIC upskilled me to become more kind and compassionate, I was starting to like my behaviour, my usual conversations with personnel initiated with a smile and lead to words like please or casual greets.

'I love the way you shower the waiters with your kindness and compassion,' complimented Subrato.

'Thank you,' I responded.

I was loving Subrato's company, he was an easy guy to be with, I wasn't regretting my decision about giving him a second chance.

'Let's order some wine,' suggested Subrato.

'I don't drink,' I updated him.

He raised his eyebrows and asked with a mischief in his cadence, 'have you ever tried drinking?' he inquired.

'Yeah. Once. I was a total mess,' I giggled retrospecting the other night. I didn't feed him with any other details and kept myself minimal.

'And what was the occasion?' Subrato asked intrigued.

'Some one ditched me,' I notified him.

'The guy has to be a maniac to ditch a sensible girl like you,' he gave me a coquettish grin.

I said nothing but giggled and my giggles grew louder shaping into laughter.

As the waiter arrived with food, I subsided laughing. The food looked so delicious that I wanted to savour my favourite concocts and forget about everything else. The waiter served us a mini portion of the delicacy and left us alone.

'Shonali,' Subrato addressed me in his peculiar Bengali accent, 'tell me more about you,' he demanded to know as he pierced fresh mustard marinated fish with a fork and ingurgitated a big piece in his mouth. If he weren't using a fork, I would have called him a desi gorb, a cute desi gorb.

'Why are you so curious to know things about me?' I countered as I separate a small part of freshly mustard marinated fish with the help of my knife and put it in my mouth with the fork, neither did my cheeks distort nor did my jaws while I masticated the delicacy. Subrato watched me closely while I was eating and he seemed to enjoy watching me eat.

'Because I'm a very picky reader and your mysterious book cover has fascinated me to my core,' he kept his fork aside and answered whimsical but sensual.

I smiled at his witty response and permitted him, 'ask me anything.'

'No, no, I don't want to fire an interrogative session on you, I just want to know your basic details like where are you from? Which school and which college did you attend?' he filled in the space between his fingers by locking his two hand and was eager to hear my response.

'I'm basically from Kolkata,' I answered.

'Same here, me too from Kolkata, Where in Kolkata are you from?' he demanded to know excitedly.

'AG block,' I answered.

'Such a small world I have spent 23 years of my life in AG block. Which street?' Subrato's excitement upsurges, if there was a pyranometer to monitor the irradiance of his excitement, then the instrument would have read as 2 W/m^2.

'4th cross road,' I announced.

Subratos face lit up, my every answer was increasing his irradiance of excitement, the calculations of my imaginary pyranometer was upsurge to 4 W/m^2. 'Are you serious? we are home town neighbours. My home is on the next street, 1st avenue street, adjacent to 4th cross road,' he gesticulated each name of the respective street articulating with his hands displaying the intensity of excitement within him.

'Wow! and we never crossed path, isn't it strange?' I marked my exclamation with a question.

'Which school were you in?' we asked in an unison. We broke out into laughter unanimously because we happened to utter same question in a exact same juncture of time.

'You go first,' he allowed me to speak first.

'Sir Aurbindo Institute Of Education,' I announced.

'That's cheating,' he playfully banged his hand on the aqua marine themed table which had tiny corals and shells embedded in it to reveal his irradiance of excitement which raised to 6 W/m^2, 'you are a resident of my block!! You went to my school!!!! You lived a street across!!!!!! And you never met me in Kolkata?? Instead you are meeting me here in Mumbai after so many years???? Why did you do this to me Shonali??????' his cadence danced in accordance with the irradiance of his excitement as he spoke in a series.

I said nothing but laughed out loud at the series of coincidences which life kept hidden from us.

'My guruji resides on your street, do you know Guruji Bhaskar Sen?' Asked Subrato.

'Is he your Guru Ji?' I countered. Now it was my time to be under the surveillance of my imaginary pyranometer to measure the irradiance of my excitement.

'Yeah, I learned music from him,' he disclosed.

My excitement level stride up to a next level, 'He is my dad,' I said after a long surprised pause.

'What???? I mean...... you uh..... you are......' the level of our irradiance of excitement leap up to cross 10 W/m^2 on my pyranometer, we couldn't utter a word out of exhilaration. I was equally baffled with the coincidences that crossed us, I could totally feel the tingles running down my veins which was probably passed on to me by him.

Our excitement was interrupted by the waiter, he arrived with desserts; the incredible mishti doi and rosogullas. We shared our desserts with each other.

•••••

Subrato paid the bill and I let him pay without dutching *#LOVETONIC 16 Let your guy, pay the bill. When he is paying the bill for you, he feels a sense of pride, don't steal the pleasure of paying for you from him.* The entire dining experience was an exciting roller coaster ride for me; at an initial point of time, my mind was occupied by thoughts of Vikram, as the time passed I started to have wonderful time with Subrato. My mind nudged me, *Shona even if you don't love Subrato now, you will eventually fall in love with him later, he is nice guy.* Sometimes you don't fall in love with a person, but you fall in love with the time you spend together.

'I still can't believe that you are my Guruji's daughter. Undoubtedly, I felt an intense connection with you on the very first day when I met you, I regret that I didn't meet you earlier, Where were you hiding all these years Shonali,' said Subrato as we walked out the restaurant.

'I was hiding in the next street,' my answer was filled with my giggles and his guffaws.

We occupied our seats in the car. We barely spoke on the way back to home, we spent time looking at each other and trying to look away from each other. We silently heard to his collection of songs, the lyrics were doing the talking between us.

Subrato applied brakes to his car at the same place where he picked me up from, the entrance of my lane. He got off the car to open the door for me, 'Shonali I had a wonderful time tonight I have never felt so connected with anyone before. Being around you presses the happiness button in me, I don't have to put an effort to be happy when I am around you,' he concluded when I got off the car and stood by him to bid an adieu.

'Thanks you so much Subrato, I too had a wonderful time with you,' I said, I turned around to leave his vicinity and walked a few steps away.

'Shonali,' he alluded me.

'Yes,' I halted and turned around to meet my gaze with his.

'Shonali, I m umm I have never,' he babbled nervously and his body squirmed, 'I mean I love you.' He revealed.

'What????' I uttered in a state of astonishment, I wasn't expecting this, 'It's too early, we have just met,' I said.

'I know it's not easy to woo a girl of high integrity and high self worth like you, but I can't help myself, I LOVE YOU,' he repeated.

I said nothing but stood there in silence.

'I'm not rushing on you, I'm prepared that you are going to take all your time to respond,' he continued, 'Remember one thing, what ever you answer is whether it's a yes or a no, I'm losing myself,' his eyes were filled with amour.

'Losing yourself, Subrato???' I demanded an explanation.

'Well, if you say a no, I'll go crazy, I'll have to take depression pills. On the other hand, if you say a yes, I'll anyway go crazy out of excitement and happiness, so I'm anyway loosing my self on you, for you, over you and you know what,'

'What???'

'I'm loving this,' he leaned in to me, came closer, his laid on mine, his lips closer to mine, he wanted to kiss me, but I identify my #LOVETONICS competently. the *#LOVETONIC 17 said,*

DON'T KISS ON FIRST DATE, no matter how scrumptious he is, no matter if you dying for building that connection, no matter if he looks deep into your eyes, no matter if your date is incomplete without a kiss, but you will not let him kiss on your first date. Beside that, don't let him hold your waist in public, he should realise that if he wants more of you, he will have to wait until you two create a deep and strong bond, more over he will have to wait for you two to be alone.

I instantly pulled my self away and bid an adieu to him. I left his vicinity and faded in the darkness of the lane.

●●●●●

#LOVETONIC 15: Don't reveal your residential address at an initial stage, even if the guy is coming over to pick you up or drop you off.

#LOVE TONIC 16: Let your guy, pay the bill. When he is paying the bill for you, he feels a sense of pride, don't steal the pleasure of paying for you from him.

#LOVETONIC 17: DON'T KISS ON FIRST DATE, no matter how scrumptious he is, no matter if you dying for building that connection, no matter if he looks deep into your eyes, no matter if your date is incomplete without a kiss, but you will not let him kiss on your first date. Beside that, don't let him hold your waist in public, he should realise that if he wants more of you, he will have to wait until you two create a deep and strong bond, more over he will have to wait for you two to be alone.

CHAPTER 16

The dalliance between Subrato and me was progressing smoothly. Though our relationship was based on mutual admiration, it was more than a casual fling to him. He was always eager and excited to see me, he always managed to extract time to talk to me in his busy schedule, he was in love with me and he always put an extra effort to express his love via certain small deeds of compassion and endearment.

I too was tending myself to be inclined towards Subrato, he filled in all the criteria in my check list of 'the man of my dreams'. Although I liked him with all my heart, I was going through a tough time while walking on the edgy way between liking him and trying to fall in love with him. I accompanied him in all the boring healthcare related seminars, fund raisers, conferences, symposiums and other meetings conducted by doctors association for upgrading and proliferation of information among doctors. I desperately wished that either I reached late on those seminars or I could carry my feather stuffed pillow and my ultra soft blanket so that I could sleep peacefully to spare myself from long sermons, but Subrato was the key speaker in most of the seminars and he expected my physical presence in order to offer my companionship to him.

Apart from medical and other health related symposiums, we went for a couple of sci-fi movies, (I am not a sci-fi movie person, I'm more of a romantic Bollywood version of entertainment seeker). To me, the sci-fi movies are nothing more than an improved version of old Hindi mythological series. I couldn't interpret the essence of those movies, the positive side of the movie hangouts was; Subrato offered me his shoulder to rest on. The other perks were; movies were followed by dinner dates or long drives which I loved.

Subrato introduced me to his mom over a video call. This gesture was a sure shot sign indicating Subrato's commitment in our relationship. *A guy introduces a girl to his parents only when he has an inkling of commitment in his mind.* His mother was a kind and compassionate woman, she was always concerned about my cooking skills, she was considerate enough to express her thoughts regarding my need to upgrade my cooking skills so that I could cook the perfect sorshe illish and macher jhol for his son. 'All mums are like that,' Subrato managed to defend neatly.

While we were out on a date, Subrato was never left alone, his phone always bleeped and ring. Umpteen number of calls flooded in from his patients, a few calls were emergency cases and the other ones were subject to be mandatorily received by him. 'I'll have to take this call, may be the patient is in a needful state,' he always defended himself and expected a high level of understanding from me. He was never indifferent but he didn't give me entire of himself as well.

Of course Subrato and me kissed each other and we caressed too, but strangely at the very point of time when I should be excited and passionate, anticipating my future with Subrato, a spark inside me rose in resistance and held me back. My doubts were minute seeds at first, but with time they took root in my mind and as the weeks passed by, they expanded into full fledged plant, nourishing itself and growing at night. Subconsciously I began to resist the path which have always been so clear for me. As Subrato and me proceeded to each new level of relationship, I felt a pressure knotted deeper in my chest. I closed the box instead of withdrawing, I chose keeping quiet rather than expressing my feelings. I started to stay aloof with every one, I dig myself into work, ADD IT TUDE going global was a perfect excuse to keep myself busy and disengage from every one. I wasn't honest enough to disclose my feelings to Subrato. Neither I revealed anything to Risha, nor did I speak about it to Vikram.

Meanwhile, a strong bond of friendship developed between Vikram and Risha, they shared almost every thing and anything with each other. One fine morning when I bumped into Risha's room, to bid my adieu to her before leaving for office, I found her sleeping peacefully. A thin sheet covered her torso, her hair spread on to the pillow, a faint smile describing calmness, played on her face. She was a grown up girl, but to me, she was my little girl, my small sister.

I quietly turned around to exit her room without disturbing her, but her buzzing phone halted me to stand still. I walked to the side table, I picked up her phone with an intention to switch it into silent mode so that Risha could sleep peacefully without any disturbance, but the name which flashed on the phone screen captured my attention, it was a text from 'Vikram'. His name intrigued me to shake my ethics. Something inside me was so incongruous that I wanted to read the texts. I contemplated Risha's phone for more than a minute, it was continuously buzzing to indicate inflow of texts and my heart was pounding heavily with every buzz. I pilfered her phone and managed to slink out of the room iniquitous, I ceased to breath for a second or two before I rushed to balcony to breathe some fresh air and I soon tabbed on Vikram's name to read the messages. I was cognizant that my action was a deceitful act towards Risha because I was reading her private texts but I couldn't resist my self.

The WhatsApp window popped to show Vikram's recent text, 'Risha I'm sorry for being rude last night, don't be mad at me for too long, you are my only buddy in the city. Come on now wake up and reply to me soon.'

I shifted my gaze away from the phone and peered at the endless destitute morning dew wet street downstairs as I thought to myself, 'Risha is mad at Vikram !!!! I need to find the reason,' so I scrolled up to check their previous night's blazed up conversation.

Vikram : 'I love her Risha, I seriously do, I have never felt like this for anyone before. She is not any other girl, she is special to me, she is important, I love her.' I could feel the intensity of his love in the text written by him. His each word described his madness and intensity in amour.

Risha: 'Tell her instead of telling me Vikram.' She scoffed.

Vikram : 'How do you expect me to tell her about my feeling when you already know that she is taken?'

I paused reading and mumbled to myself, 'That Bitchika is already engaged and has a fiancé back in her home town, yet she was deliberately messing with Vikram's life. Despite knowing the truth Vikram was playing with his own life.' I denoted as I gritted my teeth in anger, I rested my left hand on the balcony sill.

Risha: Why don't you use your LOVETONICS?

Vikram: Because I don't want to manipulate or influence her decision, I'm happy to see her happy.

Vikram was truly in love with Bitchika, he was willing to sacrifice his happiness for her happiness. How lucky she was!!! (Only if she realised)

Risha: It's not called manipulation, it's called making her realise that you love her and finding out whether she loves you. May be she loves you too, may be she herself doesn't knows that she loves you Vikram.

Vikram : Cut it Risha, I'm in a very confused state of mind, I my self don't know what should be done and what shouldn't. All I know is that I love the feeling of tingle I get when I see her smile. Her gleaming eyes make me the happiest person on the earth. I fell in love with her even before I realised that I did. Risha, now when I know that I'm in love with her I don't want to tell her about my feelings and spoil things for her. Do you understand?

Risha: No Mr. Vikram Khanna, neither I understand you, nor do you understand me. When we two don't understand each other, what is the point in being friends? Talk to me only when you understand me. Good bye.

Risha let out a stream of passive anger and concluded the conversation.

Vikram: Risha please don't be mad at me, try to understand me. Vikram pleaded but Risha didn't bother to reply.

I finished reading the conversation and kept Risha's phone aside.

The conversation was a proof that Vikram was deeply and madly in love, though he no where mentioned Deepika's name, but it was an obvious conclusion that he was in an open relationship with Deepika. Each time I stalked Deepika's Instagram, I ended up crossing new pics of the new couple, they appeared to have a gala time in all the pics. But comprehending their quintessence relationship was out of my belief system because Deepika was engaged to another boy. Her loving fiancé was waiting for her back in her home town, yet she managed to cleanly cheat on her fiancé and double date with Vikram, more over, Vikram was well aware about her engagement and relationship status, yet he involved himself in a full fledged relationship with Deepika, he definitely loved Deepika a lot.

My heart ached to see Vikram and Deepika together. Whether I accepted it or no, I shared a platonic relationship with Vikram, if at all, there were no Subrato and no Deepika in our respective lives, we had a miniscule chance of transforming our platonic relation in to a full fledged love affair. I have had felt the spark, the moment of magic with Vikram umpteen number of times. The way he cared for me, the way he looked into my eyes, the way he teased me, the way he exactly interpret the essence of my conversation even before I initiated one, every element in the air between us was amorous. Too bad, I failed to identify the potential moment of magic between me and Vikram. I was always holding my checklist about the guy of my dream, if I ever shifted my gaze away from the checklist, if I ever allowed my self to seek the fun element hidden in uncertainty rather than chasing stability and security, then, Vikram was the 'imperfectly perfect guy', but it was too late, too bad he was taken and into a happy relation with Deepika, whereas, even I was into a committed relationship with Subrato.

As a result, I managed to maintain a distance between me and Vikram to avoid awkward situations between us. I changed my route whenever Vikram was about to cross my path. He was courteous enough to smile at me when accidentally my gaze met his in the office lobby but I stayed indifferent. We barely entered a conversation like we used to. A hollow loop formed between us which was multiplying in size day be day. I couldn't figure out the reason behind my anomalous behaviour. I sat down with a pen and paper to note down things which were bothering me, the first thing in my list was; (I practice this weird but effective exercise of take down notes of things which bother me and end up destroying the list), I picked up a note pad and drew out a pen from the pen holder.

I began to trace down my thoughts onto the paper, 'Subrato =》 Subrato is exactly the kind of guy I have been looking for, he fulfils all the credentials in my check list. He is a doctor, he is handsome, he is a Bengali, he loves me, he is in a committed relationship with me,(commitment is something guys don't give easily) he is the stability and security I have always been craving for, but there is something missing between me and him. That spark, that emotional bond, that sedulous care, that mild concern is somewhere missing between me and Subrato.' I twirled a bang of my wavy hair with my pen as I began to think further, I was paying a big price for stability and security in my life. I continued scribbling on the paper to express my next concern.

'Vikram => I am not sure about my feelings for Vikram, but I am way too jealous when ever I encounter him with Bitchika. My heart undergoes an intense urge to swap myself with Deepika in pictures posted by her on Instagram, but I can't denote jealousy as love. They are into a happy relationship and I too should focus on improving things between me and Subrato rather than seeking other taken options.' I kept my pen aside and brushed my wavy hair with my right hand.

Before I could destroy the paper, the door to my cabin opened with a thud. I looked up instantly to find Vikram entering my office, 'hey Shona,' he alluded my name with a swag in his tone. That was his ishtyle. He never knocked on the door, never gave a prior warning and never asked for a permission to enter, he always ambled in with rawness. He occupied the seat in front of me.

'Hi Vikram,' I mumbled nervously. The culprit in me rapidly tore the sheet of paper to separate it from the notepad before Vikram could notice my scribbles and inquire about my nasty thoughts.

'You are wearing a nice shirt, royal blue suits you,' I complimented him to distract his attention elsewhere away from my hand written confession note.

'What are you hiding from me?' Vikram's eyebrows raised, he inquired me as he saw me crumbling the piece of paper into a waste paper ball. I failed to hide from Vikram's observant eyes despite making an effort.

'Uh umm uhm, nothing, it's just,' I babbled and shabbily defended my self.

'Show it to me,' he extended his right palm in my direction in order to demonstrate his demand.

'No,' I denied as I smiled.

'Shona, you are hiding something from me????' he got off his seat and walked past the table to reach me. 'yehi teri dosti yehi tera pyar? Beech me aa gai iss love letter ki deewar,' he mimicked a vintage humorous Hindi dialogue in a parlance used by the famous Bollywood actors from 90's silver screen.

I instantly started laughing at the mimicry and his facial expressions, 'Vikram it's personal,' I stood up in defence and held the paper ball behind my back crumbling it further rigidly between my palms.

'I know all your personal things (including that you wear sports bra), come on Shona, show it to me,' Vikram leaned in like a stubborn kid and tugged my hands rigidly. I chuckled and teased him as I escaped his grip.

The aura in my cabin was soon metamorphose into a frisky kid's play area. We entered into a frolicsome scuffle. I dodged him on my left and then on the right, I finally climbed up on my chair and raised my hand holding the note higher in the air to dodge him further. He tried all the possible options to reach on top, he applied his roguish energy to win the tussle against me and obtain the note, but failed the first attempt miserably. He tried again and climbed on the other chair to tugged my hand, I switched the note onto my other hand and managed to release myself from his grip. I got off the chair, he followed me.

'Nooooooo,' I squealed as I broke into laughter, his tickling fingers made it difficult for me to stop him for a longer span of time.

My cabin was filled with our giggles and guffaws. Vikram held me by my waist and I struggled to stagger my body until I reached window, I finally threw the paper ball out of the window, it flew in the air disappearing like a tiny dot as it dropped, 'now go and get it,' I said in a sarcasm as I gloated over my victory and laughed out loud.

'That's not fair Shona,' Vikram withdraw and released me from his grip when he accepted that he was subjugated by me. The tussle left him wheezing so he occupied a chair to grasp breath.

'Every thing is fair in love and war,' I too was panting, I reached my hand for water.

Vikram sat quietly, his derided but impish child like countenance indicated his pain in defeat.

'Vikram,' I offered him some water.

'You have changed Shona,' he commented.

'Come on Vikram grow up, they were just a few words, nothing important,' I defended my self and poured all the blame over him.

'You have changed,' he repeated as he played with the paper weight. 'you have become so indifferent, you hardly talk to me, you don't respond to my calls, you don't share anything with me anymore, it's been ages that we had a conversation. Is something bothering you Shona?' he displayed his concern. I peered at him undisturbed and shifted my gaze to my laptop.

'I'm cool Vikram,' I lied as I pretended to appear busy with my laptop, 'this ADD IT TUDE going global is eating up all my energy and time,' I cooked up a fake explanation.

'Shona,' Vikram denied accepting my lame excuse, 'is everything fine between you and Subrato?' he asked a straight question.

I said nothing but nodded a yes indifferent and dig myself into work.

'Shona, look up at me,' he commanded as he flipped closed my laptop, 'stop lying,' Vikram read my empty eyes, I shared such a relationship with him that I barely had to spell out my thoughts or complete a sentence, he comprehended my feelings even before I initiate a conversation.

'What????' I said meagre.

'You need the next #LOVETONIC,' he uttered.

'Vikram I'm fine, things are f......' I struggled to continue before he paused me and continued himself to complete my sentence.

'f#*ked up,' Vikram said out loud, 'things are actually, literally and genuinely f#*ked up, it's you who can't accept it Shona,' he peered straight into my eyes. His eye were mirror to my soul, I couldn't lie to him any further.

'Vikram,' I said.

'Shona,' he tried hard to supress his smirk.

'Okay, give me your next #LOVETONIC,' I admitted my defeat because I know that things between me and Subrato were askew and our relationship needed a repair.

'I'm glad you realise,' he left his chair, stood up and walk across the table to reach me, 'so the next #LOVETONIC,' he bent down to meet my seated height and wrapped his strong arm across my chair. My nostrils were filled with his musk, he was mere five inches away from me.

'#LOVETONIC 18: *Shonali, in your relationship with Subrato, you have compromised on your part. You have let him choose the movie, you have let him select the restaurants, you have accompanied him in his professional seminars. You have proved that you are adaptable and apt for him, Now, it is his turn to adapt himself and make compromises for you,' explained Vikram. It was difficult for me to concentrate on what he said because his closeness was a sheer distraction.* It took me half a minute to process and realise the #LOVETONIC 18.

'What do you exactly want me to do?' I moved away from him and inhaled deeply. I walked over to the window and leaned my torso by the window sill.

Vikram followed me and stood behind me, he folded his arms across his wide chest, 'I want you to test him.'

'Test???' I asked as I turned to face him and leaned my back on the sill.

'Test the degree to which he is happily willing to compromise for you,' he quoted an inverted comma in the air with his fingers when he uttered the word HAPPILY.

'And how will I do this?' I demanded to know.

'Well, you will pick up a place. You will pick up an activity which is exactly opposite to what he picks up for you. You will observe the degree to which he is offering his involvement in the activity that you choose for you two,' he paused. 'This #LOVETONIC is very important Shona, this is basically to check the level of compatibility between you two. This is about observing his willingness to accept the differences between you two,' he explained.

I said nothing but heeded him with determination while I was mentally trying to figure out a solution to my next problem. I silently turned around towards the window and peered out the endless sea.

'Shoot your next concern,' Vikram interpreted my silence so well that he was exactly aware about the dissension running in my mind.

'What do I plan for Subrato?' I said, 'I mean, which place do I pick for him, which restaurant and which activity should I choose?' I looked up at him and displayed my concern.

'I knew that this is about to come from you,' he rolled his eyes. 'Plan what ever you like Shona, follow your heart,' he suggested.

'What would you have planned if you were in my shoes?' I tried a trap to extract a few expertise ideas.

'I don't wanna try women's foot wear,' he smartly escaped.

I laughed. 'Okay, what would you have planned for me, if you were in Subrato's shoes?'

'I'm not that lucky,' said Vikram, his gaze didn't move away from me. A brief silence filled in the gap between us. He walked a step closer to me, he didn't shift his gaze from mine, neither did I dare to look away from him, 'I'm not that lucky Shona,' he repeated his words. His voice grew more sensual and intense as he drove further a step closer to me. His each step towards me was giving me collywobbles in my stomach.

'Tell me,' I insisted, my voice soft and skittish.

Vikram leaned in closer to me, 'I would have planned a picnic for you,' he looked deep in my eyes and paused to continue after a brief span, 'a long drive kind of thing followed by a short trek into the woods which would head us to a small tent house beside a scenic lake,' he said in a sequence without realising that he was mere an inch away from me, I could already see the place via Vikram's glittering eyes and imagined me with him in the picturesque location. He continued, 'I would have spent entire day listening to you and talking to you. We would have spent the evening watching the clementine setting sun while sitting outside our tent,' I half laughed and blushed. In my imaginations, I was already enjoying the clementine sunset with Vikram, he too seemed to be so lost in me that without realising he replaced past participle with future tenses, 'Shona, we will be each other with each other, without cell phones, laptops and Wi-Fi. We will enjoy the peace and serenity between us and around us.' I could feel the voice of his breath as he spoke, his eyes twinkled. 'And slowly the night will follow and we will lay under the sky contemplating the gleaming stars and our torsos wrapped in a cosy blanket and......' His words were imaginary but real, figment but assertive, undefined but articulate.

'And food?' only an illicit like me could come up with a stupid question at such a romantic moment.

'Don't worry, Swiggy delivers food every where,' Vikram was witty, humorous and romantic at a same point of time.

We laughed in an unison and contemplated each other non stop.

A gentle knock on my cabin's door hauled us back to reality from our figment romantic date.

'Come in,' I instructed as I withdraw myself from Vikram and stepped away.

That was Deepika, she sauntered into the cabin and said, 'hey Vikiiiiiii,' she addressed Vikram with his nick name, of course he was her guy.

'Hello Shonali ma'am,' she greeted me formally.

'Hello,' I answered dryly.

'Vikiiiiiii, we didn't click our selfie for the dayyyyy and you know whatttttt? I love this shirt on youuuuu,' she spoke in a snobby parlance extending the sound of the each word at the end as if she was reciting a poem.

'I guess this shirt is everybody's favourite,' Vikram shifted his gaze away from Bitchika and looked up at me.

'Come on let's click our SELFIE OF THE DAYYYYY, so that I can post it on Instagram' Bitchika held her phone with her left hand and held Vikram's arm with the right one, they smiled for the click and suddenly Deepika withdraw from Vikram and uttered,

'Wait,' she looked up at me, 'Shonali ma'am can you please click a pic for us?' she paused for my response and said when she noticed that I was blank without any response, ' I'm sure that it'll be a better click than a selfie.'

'Uhm me?' I asked lost.

'Yeah please,' she said confidently as she handed over her phone to me without waiting for my approval.

The focus of the camera rested on the duo and they appeared to be a beautiful couple, I soon clicked a picture of the two and left my cabin to avail some fresh air.

●●●●●

#LOVETONIC 18: A girl usually compromises in a relationship. You let him choose the movie, you have let him select the restaurants, you have accompanied him in his professional seminars. You have proved that you are adaptable and apt for him, Now, it is his turn to adapt himself and make compromises for you.

CHAPTER 17

It was a deviant Saturday morning at office unlike other usual holiday weekends. The event of the grand merger; MODE DE VIE with ADD IT TUDE was due on Monday hence we were left with no other option besides slogging on weekends. I was physically occupied with the preparations of the resplendent event, parallel to which, I was mentally occupied considering one after the other propositions from Subrato.

Subrato was trying all he could to arrange a great weekend for us, but nothing could impress me to my core. He recommended hundreds of *get outs* which I rejected instantly. Nothing seemed to be perfect or at all close to perfect. His ideas were as cool as going for shopping and as vague as spending a day at zoo. My expectations were high, I wasn't expecting our we time to be surrounded by caged hyenas and giraffes. I wanted to feel special, I wanted him to desire me, covet me. I wanted to analyse if he was happily willing to compromise over his comfort zone for me. My decisions would co-relatively depend on his behaviour and my anatomisation.

My phone bleeped again to indicate a text received from Subrato, I sneaked a moment from my laptop and promptly tabbed on my phone to give a quick look to his text.

'How about a day escape at this resort?' the text was followed by a series of picturesque images of a swanky resort surrounded by mountains high above the boulder. The locus was a serene landscape alongside a natural lake. A hot infinity pool merged with the lake which extended to the mountains, it was a beautiful place to spend a day with your love. Another image displayed horses, canoes, row boats, countless walks around the lake and the property which exhibit the numerous activities we could indulge ourselves in.

'Appears promising,' I shut my laptop and leaned my back on the comfortable rotating chair to enjoy a small hiatus from work. 'The place looks like a combination of serenity and adventurous activities,' I replied.

While Subrato was typing a reply I quickly tabbed on my Instagram new feeds. I wasn't exactly addicted to Instagram or any other social media site but I have been spending my past couple of days checking on my Instagram new feeds. This task was suddenly included in the list of my mandatory *things- to-do*, the reason behind this obnoxious behaviour was as simple as *I was in an urgent need to espy on Deepika and Vikram's latest pictures.* I scrolled down the Instagram new feeds to get a glimpse of their fresh new SELFIE OF THE DAY. I spot the pic where Vikram was holding Bitchika, *holding like not casual holding but like he was holding her real close to himself.* Jealousy creeped in my heart making it's way to every nerve in my body. The photograph appeared as if it has been clicked right after a passionate kiss. Blood in my veins boiled to its maximum temperature and I couldn't breath appropriately, I needed to get my eyes out of the picture, I needed to get rid of malevolent jealousy, I needed to get rid of Vikram Bitcika and their amorous affair, I needed to escape the Instagram app. In devastating anger, I held tab and uninstalled the Instagram app instantly and banged my phone on the desk fiercely. I resumed leaning back on the chair like a phlegmatic stone. I peered at the lord Buddha grey acrylic painting which was hanging peacefully on the red wall.

Within seconds my phone bleeped to indicate a text received from Subrato, I swapped the widget to read it. 'The resort values its guests by referring to various activities they engage and depict themselves as active organisers of paddle boating, kayaking, horse riding. The executive suite which I'm planning to opt has a Jacuzzi right in the suite, so you see, we can relax after the tiring, adventurous and fun day. I'm waiting for your approval,' appeared Subrato's text followed by tonnes of exhilarating emoticons, he sounded super excited. I scrolled up to see the promotional images, the Jaccuzi was occupied by a lovey dovey couple, A handsome model held a girl who was accoutred in a sizzling hot lingerie. I stopped for a while and entered into a conflict with my own self;

My heart: Shona don't you think this is a zeitgeber that your relationship with Subrato is going to next level. This is an alarm bell, this is sharp warning, snooze him a NO.

My mind: The next level implies physical intimation. It implies you'll have to go shopping and find the sexiest lingerie in the town.

My heart: It isn't about lingerie you fool. It's about your relationship with Subrato is moving to next level. Are your prepared for it? Do you really love Subrato? Is your inclination towards Subrato restricted to the checklist of the criteria which he fulfils.

My mind: Of course you love Subrato. Don't waste time on Vikram, he is taken plus he doesn't fulfils any of your criteria. You love Subrato.

My heart: If you really love Subrato then why does your heart skips a beat when Vikram is around you? Why do you feel jealous when Vikram is with Deepika? Why did you uninstall your Instagram to devoid yourself from their pictures? What is the sweet awkwardness you feel when Vikram is around you?

I sink into my chair unwavering, submerged into the ocean of nauseous question marks until my phone bleeped to indicate a text received from Subrato, 'I'm waiting for your approval, I'll make the bookings as soon as you approve.'

I soon typed a reply, 'Subrato, I have to join office on Monday morning at sharp 8, hope you remember that the merger event in on Monday, you have to keep the schedule in mind before finalizing any bookings.'

'I have scheduled everything don't you worry. This resort is located in the pristine outer skirts of Mumbai around the Sahyadri mountain ranges, it is barely at a distance of 40 kilo-metres from Mumbai, so as per my plan, we will leave from Mumbai on Sunday; which is tomorrow at sharp 6 in morning and we will reach the resort in two hours which will leave us with an entire day and night speech spend with each other. On Monday, we will check out at sharp 5 A.M in the morning and reach Mumbai latest by 7 o clock in the morn. I'll drop you dir-ectly at the office,' Subrato sounded so excited that repudiating him wasn't an option left with me.

'Sounds good,' I typed. I anyway much needed an escape from Vikram and Deepika. Vikram was capriciously taken and I couldn't find an appropriate reason to deny Subrato. Subrato was trying all he could to step out of his comfort zone for me, he definitely deserved a chance. 'Yes, go for it, make the bookings,' I soon typed and sent.

The moment I sent the text to Subrato, Vikram made his raw entry into my cabin. I kept the phone aside and heeded him, he looked upset unlike his usual comportment.

'There is a problem Shona,' he announced. His forehead creased into tubular rigid with worry. There was something quintes-sential about him which made him appear strong, self con-tained and even more handsome each time I saw him. I resisted my urge to run my fingers over his creased forehead and tried to pay attention to his plight.

'What is wrong Vikram ?' I inquired hiding my impulsive desire behind a question mark.

Vikram occupied a seat opposite to mine, 'Our leading lady, the one who is suppose to deliver the sitar performance, has met with an accident,' he blurted the predicament in one breath.

Anxiety overtook me, but instead of panicking, I chose to keep my calm and said, 'talk to the event manager, I'm sure we will find a replacement,' I came up with a very casual solution.

'No luck. We can not find a replacement in such a short notice. Not happening Shona,' tiny droplets of sweat formed along the creases of his forehead.

'I'm sure there must be a solution, think of something,' I said trying my best to focus on the predicament instead of vesting my focus onto his handsome face, 'should we cancel the sitar performance and instead opt for something else?' I suggested.

'Don't you remember vividly? Anuvind Khanna was very adamant about the sitar performance. It is very significant for MODE LA VIE, it is more about their family culture and tradition. They always initiate a new venture by offering their tribute to Goddess Saraswati in the form of a sitar performance. No way, we can't cancel it,' Vikram reminded me.

'So what do we do now?' I asked desperately seeking for a solution. I glanced into his eye for a second or two, that nanosecond gave birth to strong covetous desire, how I'd wish that he was single.

I managed to forcefully shut the second thoughts running in my mind and tried to focus on the current predicament.

'I have a solution,' he said as he stood up and walked towards the edge of my cabin, he halt by the cast glass window and peered at the never ending ocean.

'Tell me,' I demanded to know as I followed his league and stood behind him.

'You,' he turned around and shifted his gaze away from the sea to look up at me expectantly.

'Me????' I utter in shock, my eyebrows raised.

'Yes, you. You play sitar and you can deliver an awesome performance,' he said confidently. His eyes unwavering from mine.

'No way Vikram,' I displayed my discountenance swivelling my eyes between him and the grey lord Buddha painting on the adjacent red wall.

'This is the only way Shona,' he persuaded.

'No Vikram,' I said adamantly and looked out of the window towards the ocean reminiscing the past ignominious event of my life when I witnessed a failure in delivering a sitar performance during my college days.

'Yes Shona,' he argued strongly.

My phone bleeped again and it distracted my attention away from the plight. I reached for my phone.

'What is it Shona?' Vikram followed me towards the desk and inquired.

'Oh nothing,' I didn't give it much weight.

'Tell me,' he coerced.

'Subrato has come up with a perfect plan for our perfect weekend,' I announced carrying a half smile and leaning my body weight on the desk.

'That sounds nice, what is the plan?' he demanded to know.

'Look at this,' I tabbed open my WhatsApp and turned my phone towards him to show him the pictures.

'Nice, but don't you think you should postpone,' Vikram gave me a quick glance, 'I mean don't take me wrong but the pressure of event and so many other important things are on the way,' he displayed his disconcert and moved away from me.

'I wish I could postpone, but Subrato is traveling to Kolkata next week.' I tried to explain, 'Vikram, this place is barley at a distance of 40 kilometres from Mumbai, so I have planned a scheduled to return Mumbai before the event.' I moved a step towards him.

'I know you are very responsible Shona but,' he sounded unexpectedly unconvinced.

'But what?' I inquired looking deep into his eyes.

'I mean, uhm,' Vikram babbled, he sounded jittery, he stole away his gaze from me as he continued, 'Shona, Subrato hasn't made a commitment to you, I think it's too early for a night out' he expressed his discountenance trying his maximum to maintain his composure.

So the actual problem is spending a night with Subrato.

'Come on Vikram I'm not a teenager, I'm an adult and Subrato isn't a stranger, he is my boyfriend and all couples do spend quality time with each other. I think you are over thinking,' I rebuked as I moved away from him towards the adjacent wall, trying to sound as unostentatious as I could.

'I'm not over thinking it's just I'm a bit possessive about you,' he followed me aggravate and uttered his sharp annoyance, his voice went high.

Possessive about me? What do you mean by that Mr. Vikram, can you please give me a precise definition for your possessiveness. Does it means that you love me possessiveness or does it mean only possessive possessiveness?

'What do you mean?' I raised my eyebrows to question him as I turned towards him facing him directly. I looked into his eyes all I could see was rage and resentment.

That was the first time I saw Vikram losing his cool. Somewhere deep inside me I was liking his *possessiveness* towards me.

'I mean, I mean Shona,' he struggled for words. He was fighting between the fine line; trying hard to maintain his composure and trying not so hard to loose his temper.

'Shona *#LOVETONIC 19 is that, the girl who keeps the guy waiting for sex until she is into a committed relationship, is more likely to have a healthy long lasting relationship.'*

I said nothing but looked deep into his eyes for more than a minute still trying to figure out the reason behind his possessiveness. I saw love hidden in there but he quickly veiled it with sneer.

'Vikram see this article, the couple who tend to spend night outs and are higher on the side of intimacy on dates are likely to be more committed than the couple who don't indulge themselves into each other.' I picked up an old edition article and showed it to Vikram, 'Come on, which century are you living in? It's perfectly fine to get physical before marriage. Everyone does it,' I said.

'What rubbish this article is,' he chuck the edition fiercely on the floor without giving it a glance and lost his composure, he yelled wildly. 'You are not everyone or anyone Shona,' he came closer to me I stepped behind, his masculine musk was driving me crazy, 'you are someone, someone very special,' he kept on coming closer, I kept on shifting behind until my back was pressed into the wall, 'you are different, you are pure, you are you,' our eyes were still locked, 'Why do you want to follow others when you can create your own path?' concupiscence sizzled in the air between us. Vikram pulled me close, I pushed myself away, 'You are not going for an over night with Subrato,' his voice sensuous, he sounded like he owned me, like he possessed me, like he had his rights reserved over me, somewhere I was loving and coveting for this side of Vikram, but I was still in a dilemma. Was his possessiveness a sheer concern or was it more than just being concerned?

'I have already told him a yes, bookings are done,' I informed him.

The moment Vikram heard my words, he blazed in anger, his eyes were blood shot red. It tore his heart to know what my words were doing to him. He grabbed my upper arms and dug his fingers until it hurt, He came even more closer, his eyes unmoved from mine as he uttered perturbed, his forehead cringed in anger, 'Didn't you hear me? I said you are not going for an over night with Subrato, this is final. We are not arguing over this any more,' his lips were mere an inch away from mine, his voice obsessed and sensuous, his touch was strongly electrifying me. Every cell in my body responded to the scintillating spark amidst us. Though his fingers were bruising me, hurting me but there was an edge of oneness and belongings in his touch, 'I am not letting you spend a night with him,' with each word he spoke, he came even more closer to me. He was just about to kiss me, intoxicating, passionate and deep, but at the very same point of time we heard a knock.

Vikram withdraw himself and released my arms from his grip, he fetched his senses and allowed me to fetch mine, 'come in,' he commanded.

        Deepika ambled into my cabin oblivious, her hands were piled up with files. Her intrusion hauled me back to reality from the sultry moment with Vikram, the reality where Vikram is in a healthy relationship with Deepika. The reality where Vikram wasn't mine. I lost my composure and yelled at her in frustration, 'Deepika, please leave, we are in the middle of a conversation.'

'Oh I'm sorry Shonali ma'am, I'll come later,' she left hurriedly.

'Shona, this is not the way you are, this is not the way you talk to your staff,' said Vikram as he moved away from me.

'Vikram What exactly your problem is?' my response was harshly audacious, 'that I was rude to your girlfriend?' I stood in an akimbo. I wasn't liking the new me. Love does such things to you. You suddenly become someone else and you can easily find reasons to hate yourself. I looked away from Vikram and continued talking to him impudently, 'The entire office knows about the hot scene between Deepika and you.' I paused for a brief span of time while he contemplated me in bewilderment, I swallowed hard as I spoke pretending to be unaffected by their relationship, 'Deepika is anyway your personal life and I don't want to intrude into your private zone, unlike you, Vikram.' he was left baffled, he couldn't utter a word. 'Let's keep it simple, I don't interfere in your personal life so I don't expect your interference in mine. Hope you respect my privacy.' Vikram couldn't believe my blatant implausible words. I could sense that he was hurt, but I was hurt too to see him with Deepika. I continued to blurter out, 'Vikram, I guess you forgot that Subrato was only a deal between you and me, to use your precise word, it was DEALOGICAL between you and me. You helped me to get Subrato and now it's my turn to pay off. I promised to you that I'll not only make you permanent but I will also grant you with a promotion, so I'll soon draft a promotion letter and mail it to you,' I said. Vikram looked up at me as if I ripped him into pieces tearing him apart from his earth.

I paused waiting for him to respond but he couldn't fetch words to utter. He stood unmoved and thunderbolt. The air between us was burning in fire. I couldn't meet my gaze with him, I didn't realise that our conversation would take a rough untrodden road.

Vikram spoke after an extended contemplation, 'Shonali ma'am,' he paused to take a breath. That was the first time ever he addressed me as *Shonali ma'am* instead of calling me Shona. Shonali ma'am sounded strange from his mouth. 'I almost forgot about the DEAL between us, thanks for reminding me,' he said groggily holding a lump in his throat. His voice heavy and wobbly, 'but I guess you forgot the deal. The precise deal was; if Subrato doesn't makes a commitment to you then I quit the job.'

His words were followed by long silence amid us. I tried to my maximum limit to break the silence between us and reverse things but I couldn't utter a word, I stood like an iron statue. It was his turn to speak and mine to listen, 'Subrato hasn't officially proposed to you yet, so I quit Shonali ma'am. I'll soon draft my resignation and mail it to you,' he gave me his last look and left.

●●●●●

#LOVETONIC 19 says that the girl who keeps the guy waiting for sex until she is into a committed relationship, is more likely to have a healthy long lasting relationship.'

CHAPTER 18

I don't believe that Vikram actually quit the job. I should have asked him to stay, I should have kept my ego aside and stopped him from leaving. If at all I hadn't argued with him, things would haven't turned out to be so ugly. I wasn't at peace.

Nasty thoughts occurred to me sequentially as I sat on a bench by the edge of the serene lake which was located in the swanky property of the resort. Vikram and me were the two sides of a same coin, distinct yet attached to each other. I was missing him like I was missing the other half of my body. I was empty without him. I was incomplete without him.

'Hey, you enjoying?' intruded Subrato as he returned from a horse ride. He appeared to be tired.

'Yeah, I'm enjoying. How was the horse ride?' I asked indifferent, still lost in my own thoughts.

'It was awesome, you should have joined me' he answered. My date which was supposed to be 'perfect' was actually perfect with a slight imperfection, the only imperfect things was 'ME'. I didn't involve in any of the activities. Subrato tried enough to please me, but my response was zero.

I quietly continued to peer at the lake.

'Isn't the view scenic?' he said as he placed the saddle aside and occupied a seat beside me on the iron cast bench.

SONAM KESWANI

'It's beautiful,' I contemplated the invigorating lake.

'You look disturbed is everything fine?' asked Subrato. I stood up to stroll along the lake line promenade, Subrato came along with me and walked by my side.

'Yup, I'm fine.' I looked up at him, ' it's just that the event is up tomorrow and we don't have a sitar performer.' I displayed a fake reason behind my stray comportment. Subrato tried to hold my hand but I withdrew my palms off his grip and folded my arms in an akimbo.

'Don't worry, I'm sure Vikram will find a solution, he is competent enough to manage these petty things.' I didn't dare to disclose with Subrato that Vikram had quit the job.

'Vikram suggested that I should replace the sitar performer.' I announced.

'But you don't want to perform after what happened in college, right?' he uttered bluntly.

'How do you know about it?' I halt and asked him baffled. Soft zephyr blowing across the lake embraced my hair causing it fall over my cheek.

'Your baba was my music teacher, you forgot?' he halt and looked up at me, 'I was kind of his pet, he shared almost every thing with me.' Subrato satirized to add fuel to my indignation.

'So he discussed my embarrassments with you,' I said in dismay. I couldn't believe that baba discussed the most embarrassing situation of my life with one of his students. I was burning in the fuel of exasperation.

'I don't think you should agree on doing this stage performance thing, because you have already embarrassed baba once,' advised Subrato as ran his finger around my cheek and tucked a strand of hair behind my ear.

I said nothing but glared at Subrato, I tried to fill in the gap between *the guy who fulfilled the criteria in my vacuous checklist (Subrato)* and on the other hand *the guy who stood by me in all the weird circumstances(Vikram)*. There was a huge difference in the perception of Subrato and Vikram. Vikram not only supported me, but also motivated me to go ahead and take a lead, unlike Subrato.

After a long nonchalant contemplation I left Subrato's vicinity aggravated and strolled towards the suite. Subrato followed me.

The moment I unlocked the suite and entered in, my anger disappeared like a bubble, I was bedazzled to see the heart shaped arrangements of lavenders and rose all around the room. Scented candles were placed on the side tables and centre table. A bottle of wine and two glasses rested in a corner. Chocolate dipped monochrome strawberries were waiting for me in a white platter. I forgot everything and all I could see was Subrato's efforts to please me. He did more than needed.

'I wanted to surprise you,' Subrato leaned his chin on my right shoulder, hugged me from behind and whispered in my ear.

'This is beautiful Subrato, thank you for all this,' I appreciated his effort.

'Come,' he held my hand and walked me towards the white platter of monochrome patterned chocolate dipped strawberries. 'Close your eyes,' he commanded.

The moment I closed my eyes, Vikram's chiselled face appeared in front of me. I was in a perfect moment with my perfect guy but I couldn't concentrate on anything beside Vikram, because all that I had in my mind was Vikram. I couldn't think of anyone else beside him, I couldn't do anything else beside thinking of him. It seemed like he was the only and dominant thought running in my mind. I suddenly opened my eyes to find Subrato kneeling in front of me.

'Marry me Shonali,' he held a strawberry in his hand and proposed to me.

Who the hell on earth proposes with a strawberry ??? I said nothing but glanced at the strawberry in an ambivalence of astonishment and bewilderment.

'I'm waiting Shonali, say something,' said Subrato while he was still kneeling and holding the strawberry.

'Strawberry???' I uttered, my eyebrows raised.

'Oh I'm so sorry,' he opened the strawberry which was actually a sweet strawberry shaped trinket box it had a beautiful diamond ring waiting for me inside its satin case.

'Marry me Shonali,' he repeated his proposal.

That was the moment I have been longing for. Everything I ever wanted was right in front of me, but I wasn't happy, I wasn't at peace, I closed my eyes and Vikram's *#LOVETONICS 20 reverberated in my ears; follow your heart Shona, do what you feel is right, believe in yourself, believe in your gut instinct, ask yourself what is good for you, think about your happiness, keep yourself ahead of anyone. Life isn't about escaping from others Shona, it's about finding yourself.*

I opened my eyes folded my arms and stood in an akimbo, 'Subrato get up please,' I asked him to stand up straight. 'I'm sorry Subrato, but this can't go ahead.' I admitted.

'What???' Subrato asked perplexed. 'Why??? We are so good together.'

'I can't explain. Certain things are way beyond explanation. I'm sorry.' I said.

'Shonali, I think u are having a bad day, we should keep this for some other day,' said Subrato still holding the strawberry trinket ring case in his hand.

'No Subrato, it isn't a bad day, it is a beautiful day indeed. Today I didn't lose you Subrato, instead I found myself. Good bye Subrato.' I said confidently and turned to leave.

'Shonali,' he followed me. 'Shonali, listen to me,' he appeared restless.

I halt at the door, 'Subrato, I'm sorry you are hurt but....' my heart was filled with guilt. I was guilty to hurt Subrato. He loved me, he planned things for me, he stood right in front of me with a ring and I was hurting him in return.

Subrato held my hand swiftly between his palms, 'Shonali, don't do this to me, please don't leave. We are beautiful together. We will make a lovely home. You are totally my types. My mom too likes you or else she would have never agreed on my decision of proposing to you and I would have never proposed to you if she would have disagreed. I'm sure I will never again find a girl who could please my mom like you did,' uttered Subrato.

'What?' I asked bewildered, 'you would have never proposed to me if your mom...' my guilt vanished in a second or two. 'I wish your mom never agreed upon me.' I said and left his vicinity without pausing.

'Where are you going? At least let me drop you home,' alluded Subrato. I ignored him and left without uttering a word.

●●●●●

I tried calling Vikram multiple times while I was on my way back to home in a cab, but his phone was switched off. I tried fetching his whereabouts details from Risha, Kartik and Deepika but none of them could quench my curiosity.

I entered into a jittery colloquy with my own self, where I was asking absurd questions to my own imbecile self and was trying to find the answers; *I'm sure the cab driver might have assumed me to be an escaper of a mental asylum.*

'I don't know if at all I can find him again?' was my first dumb question.

'I'm sure you will converge him at some juncture Shona,' was the answer.

'How will I face him if I ever encounter him? *I have hurt him more than anyone else could have ever hurt him.*' Was my second doltish question.

'I think you should just smile apologetically, don't utter a single word,' the answers reverting from my inner consciousness were even more doltish than the questions.

'What will I say when I meet him?'

'Be honest and say YOU LOVE HIM. Come on Shona it's high time to admit the truth. The truth is that you love him. You have loved him always and you have loved only him.' I peered out of the window still trying to sort out things running in my mind.

No sooner did I reached home, than I hugged my pillow tightly and cried, I cried like a baby, I cried like I never did before, I cried because things were crystal clear in front of me. I cried because I probably lost Vikram even before I could get him. I lost him forever, his phone was switched off he left the job and I had no inkling of his whereabouts. I lost the catalyst who helped me in finding myself.

•••••

#LOVETONICS 20 follow your heart, do what you feel is right, believe in your self, believe in your gut instinct, ask your self what is good for you, think about your happiness, keep yourself ahead of anyone. Life isn't about escaping from others, it's about finding yourself.

CHAPTER 19

It was the day of the event, I woke up with swollen red eyes and lump in my throat. My phone was on silent mode so I missed umpteen number of calls from Kartik.

No sooner did I return to his calls, than he blared out, 'Shonali, where are you?' his voice was anxious and jittery.

'Kartik,' I replied groggily.

'You won't believe Shonali, I received an email from Vikram today in the morning and the subject says RESIGNATION in bold letters,' Kartik sounded shocked and upset, 'Vikram wasn't holding a permanent position so he could quit without a prior notice,' he continued with regret, 'how are we going to manage the merger event without him?'

'Breathe in Kartik,' I obviously wasn't shocked by the news so I tried to calm him down, 'did you try calling him up?' I asked him as I got off my bed and headed towards my wardrobe to find an appropriate outfit for me.

'His phone is switched off ever since Saturday. How could he be so irresponsible? I don't believe that Vikram has done this to us,' Kartik sounded apprehensive, aggravated and worn out.

'Don't worry Kartik, I'll be there in next fifteen minutes,' I soon drew out a solid black kurta which was embellished with a red silk hemline.

'Shonali, we don't have a sitar performer,' he updated me.

'Don't worry, we have one,' I assured him and hanged the call before he could ask further details.

•••••

Maria sprayed my hair with some hair spray and brushed my face with a bronzer to highlight my cheekbone. She streaked my eyes with a dark kohl and put on a dark shade of lip gloss on my lips. She put a little too much on but I didn't care, I was too nervous to get up on the stage and perform. I wish that Vikram were somewhere around me to motivate me and uplift me, but he was no where.

'Shonali are you sure, you can do this?' asked Kartik as he walked into the green room. I looked up at his reflection casted on the full length mirror, he appeared jittery.

Even though I didn't had a confident answer to his question I somehow managed to nod a yes. Strangely, the strength to nod a yes came into me from Vikram, I could feel his essence within me. I missed him like he was a quintessential part of me. I was empty without him.

When I stepped on the stage, my heart was pounding beneath my chest, my palms were sweaty and cold, I was jittery and petrified. I felt a sharp wobble inside my stomach exactly above my navel which was an indication that I was fearful, excited and nervous all at a same point of time. I didn't dare to make an eye contact with the audience.

I froze.

I wasn't sure what to do but I thought I'd better do something, so I took a deep breath and pulled myself along, I occupied my seat by my sitar held it in my hand and closed my eyes. Vikram's words echoed in the inner of my ear tympanum as I started playing along, '*Shona, FEAR is something which is not yet happened, it might happen or may not happen. You are holding yourself back from something which may not happen at all. At least give it a try Shona,'* all I had in my mind was him. I played on.

I couldn't believe that I was playing on and on and on uninterrupted. I opened my eyes when I heard huge applauds and the applauds were not dying any sooner. I wish Baba had been there. I wish Vikram had been there.

As soon as I finished my stage performance, greeted the audience and left the stage, I hear the screechy sound of a microphone being turned on. I swivel around and it's only about five feet away on a small podium, which I hadn't noticed. A debonair in a black trouser suit taps the microphone and says, 'Ladies and gentlemen. May I have your attention please?' After a moment, he says more loudly, 'People! It's time for the speeches! The quicker we start, the quicker they're over. So, here we are!' The debonair spreads his arms. 'Welcome to this celebration of the merger, MODE DE VIE, and the wonderful ADD IT TUDE. This is a marriage of hearts and minds as much as companies, and we have many, many people to thank. Our managing director, Anuvind Khanna, showed the initial vision which led to us standing here now.'

Anuvind Khanna dressed up in a pale suit walks onto the podium, smiling modestly and shaking his head, and everyone started clapping, including me.

'Shona di you rocked the stage,' Risha's voice reached my left ear at the very same point of time I received a text from Baba. It was a strange moment for me because Baba never texted me, he always called. The text read as, 'I'm so proud of you my child, I saw your sitar performance video, Risha just sent me.'

My joy knew no bounds. I couldn't utter a single word out of exhilaration. I turned towards Risha and hugged her tight, 'Thank you so much for sending the video to Baba,' tiny droplet of tears rolled on my cheeks.

'Vikram instructed me to record your video and send it to Baba,' informed Risha.

I couldn't move for a second or two, my senses went numb when I heard his name, 'where is he?' I inquired.

'I don't know,' she said, 'may be Deepika has the answer,' she pointed towards Deepika who stood in a corner fidgeting with her phone.

'Deepika where is Vikram ?' I rushed towards her and asked.

'Shonali ma'am, you were awesome on the stage,' she ignored my question.

'Thanks. Where is Vikram ?' I repeated my question.

'Shonali ma'am I need to let you know something about me and Vikram,' she intrigued me.

'What?' I asked bemused.

'Me and Vikram are not into any scene. He was just helping me out,' she confronted.

'Helping you??' I asked baffled.

'Yeah. My fiancé was cheating on me with some other girl. Vikram planned a trap to make him jealous so that my fiancé comes back to me,' she admitted, 'those selfies of the day, those hangouts were all a part of that insane plan.'

I said nothing but heeded her as she continued, 'Vikram left the job because he couldn't bear you with Subrato, the way you couldn't bear him with me.'

'He doesn't loves you?' I asked timid

'You know better whom does he loves,' replied Deepika. I looked up at her seeking answer to my questions in her eyes. I knew the answer in my heart but before I could grasp on things disclosed by Deepika, Kartik intruded between us and interrupted my conversation with Deepika.

'Shonali, I need to talk to you for a moment,' Kartik grabbed me by hand and drew me away from Deepika.

I was still lost in the words mentioned by Deepika. My mind was trying hard to interpret the syllables. I wanted to conclude the incomplete conversation with Deepika but Kartik stood in front of me distressed. I collected my wits and responded to his presence, 'Kartik,' I looked up at him, he appeared jittery.

'You won't believe Shonali,' he said, 'Vikram is,' he paused.

'What??' I asked intrigued.

'Vikram is Anuvind's nephew,' he announced the news.

'What?' I asked shocked.

'Yes,' he confirmed, ' he is Vikram Khanna, Anuvind Khanna's nephew, the man behind the MODE DE VIE.'

'How do you know this?' I asked uncertain.

'Mr. Anuvind Khanna revealed the secret,' enlightened Kartik, 'neither did Vikram needed the job nor the promotion.'

One after the other revelations about Vikram were shaking my core off, each revelations were coming to me sequentially one after the other before I could collect myself from the previous one. I was lost among the crowd in the party.

'Mr. Anuvind Khanna wants to have a word with you,' informed Kartik.

'With me?' I asked unsure.

'He is coming here,' Kartik looked up at Anuvind Khanna who was heading towards us, 'Answer him with modesty and use your wits.' Kartik warned me before he left me alone with Mr. Anuvind Khanna.

'You must be Shonali right?' inquired Mr. Anuvind Khanna.

'Yes sir,' I answered timid.

'Vikram told me a lot about you.' He held his phone in his left hand and a glass of champagne in the right one. 'Shonali, he may not fit in to your checklist, but he is a nice guy,' he spoke as we strolled an exit off the party.

Screw the checklist.

'He isn't happy without you,' informed Mr. Anuvind.

Nor am I happy without him.

I said nothing but listened to him carefully. I wasn't comfortable with confronting my feelings for Vikram before his uncle.

'Where is he?' I gathered courage and asked.

'He is flying to London today,' he answered. I felt a heavy stone pounding on my heart.

'Can you please call him up for me? I wish to talk to him one last time.' I requested.

'He switched off his phone.'

'What time is his Flight?' I inquired.

'5.55 PM ,' informed Mr. Anuvind Khanna.

I peered at my wrist watch it showed 4.44 PM

'Thanks,' I expressed my gratitude in an utmost formal tone and left his vicinity as soon as I could.

'Hope you reach airport before time, because once he leaves India, he is never coming back.'

I'm not letting him leave India.

I drove like a maniac on the busy streets. The Google map suggested that highway would take me to the international airport from Bandra Kurla complex in fifty five minutes where as the subway would consume forty minutes. I obviously chose the subway route, because I wanted to reach airport before Vikram could. The song by Brandi Carlile amplified at a high volume over the music system in my car. 'I crossed all the lines, I broke all the rules but baby, I broke them all for you.......' Each word of the lyric was totally correlated to my situation. I was actually crossing all the red lines and I was breaking all the rule. The truth is love hold no rules.

I was stuck in traffic, I peered at my wrist watch, it showed 5.05 PM. Roads on both the sides were packed jam due to a Minister's rally. The air around me was filled with the zest of election campaign. I honked horn non stop and prayed to God for the road clearance. Nothing seemed to be working for me. God was testing my patience at every possible level.

Another fifteen minutes passed by with no trace of movement in the traffic. I looked at my left and right, forth and back, time was passing by and every passing second was pulsating my heart to beat faster.

At 5.20 PM a gleaming ray of light gave me life. It was an ambulance ambling past from behind with its buzzing siren killing the traffic. I had never in my life been so happy to see an ambulance. The traffic got cleared instantly and as I followed the ambulance to match the speed of my car with it. I covered a considerable distance by 5.30 PM. I kept driving behind the ambulance uninterrupted until it took a left turn where as my destination was on right. The moment I took a sharp right turn at the speed of 80 km/hr, I hit on a pole smashhhhh...... My head hit the steering wheel with a sharp jerk leaving my forehead hurt. A scar over my right eyebrow was bleeding out of injury causing a minor pain to me. I looked up at the injury on the rear view mirror and cleaned it with my handkerchief. 'No Shona no, you can't let this stop you.' I said to myself. People engirdled my car to help me out. I caused a minor damage to my car too, but I peered at the crowd and mumbled in a subconscious state that, 'I'm fine, thank you,' I shift the gear on the reverse mode and got back on the road only to find that I was running out of fuel. I was in static situation. I peered at my wrist watch again, it showed, 5.45 PM. I couldn't exactly figure out how would I cover a distance of twenty two minutes in mere ten minutes without fuel in my car.

I got off fiercely to find a cab, but couldn't find a single empty cab due to rally. *Just one empty cab God, please just one cab.*

'Airport please,' I waved off to an empty cab driver who denied politely. 'Ma'am, you will find a cab for airport on the opposite road.'

I realised that I should cross the subway to find a cab. I mindlessly crossed the road like a wayward child without checking out the automobiles driving towards me, two of the cars managed to save me from catastrophic accidents. *Love does these things to you, you don't give a damn of your own life. Suddenly your very precious life becomes cheap.* My hunt for cab resumed as I collected my wits and continued with my mission; *Mission getting my Vikram back.* No trace of a empty cabs, the one which were empty denied going to airport.

I peered at my watch, it showed 5.50 PM. I was merely ten minutes away from my destination, I could practically see the dome of the airport across the street hidden behind. *Run Shona run. At least you won't regret in future, at least you are making an attempt to stop him from going away. At least you know that you are running for what you want.*

I took off my stilettoes and zoomed off. I knew that it was impossible to cover a distance of ten minutes in half the time but at least I was trying and hoping for a miracle.

I reached airport and halt panting at the departure gate. I peered at my watch it showed 6. 05. PM. I knew that I lost the race but I didn't want to give up. 'Ma'am, has the flight for London left?' I asked the lady officer dressed in khaki saree uniform, who was busy scrutinizing the passports and other personal identification documents of the travellers who stood in a queue to enter the airport.

She said nothing but granted me a suspicious look, (obviously I was panting and holding my stilettoes in my hand). After a moment or two, she shrugged indifferent and replied *managing take off flights is none of my business.*

Use your wits Shona its 6.10 PM. He left.

I stood aside dismayed. I wished for the things between me and Vikram to turn out beautifully rather than taking this ugly shape. I could have made it on time if at all the road was clear and destitute of the election rally. I was mindlessly cursing the rally and the election campaign. I was left with nothing but assumptions, suppositions and memories.

I took a seat near by a pole outside the departure gate. Nothing occupied my mind, I was blank with no thoughts and no feelings left within me. I just sat there helpless and mindless. I sat in dismay and despair.

I mindlessly peered at cars coming by the departure, dropping people, unloading luggage, bidding adieu to loved one, hugging, kissing, crying, hopes to meet again, happy, sad. Airports are a hub to all the emotions merging at one place. What were my emotions? What was I feeling? I was feeling empty and lost. I was feeling hopeless. Tears rolled down my eyes, I couldn't wall them inside me anymore. I rested my elbows on my lap and covered my face with my hands. *Love does these things to you. Love is not only blind, love is also shameless.* I cried irrespective of presence of thousands of people around me at a public place.

Suddenly a familiar voice reached my ear tympanum, when my eyes were still covered with my palms, 'Shona, what are you doing here?' I looked up instantly knowing exactly who it was.

'Vikram,' I stood up immediately and wiped my tears off. *Was I dreaming? Was it a hallucination? Was he actually standing right in front of me in real?*

'You were flying to London?' I kept my illusionary thoughts aside and asked him in disbelief.

'I missed my flight, I was stuck in traffic due to a stupid election campaign,' he said with dismay. A wave of smile ran across my face. Suddenly I was grateful to the same rally, I was cursing an hour ago. My tiredness washed away, I was feeling full of life once again.

Vikram placed his rucksack aside and said with a pinch of hope in his eyes. 'What are you doing here?' he asked.

I'm here for you fool. Things were ironical and paradoxical, I saved myself from all the possible catastrophic situations, I fought the traffic, I ran across the streets holding my stilettoes in my hands like a maniac, I ended up crying in the middle of the crowd just to see him for one last time and now when he was right in front of me, I didn't exactly know what to blurter out.

'Vikram,' I finally uttered.

He looked up at me with unanticipated eyes and continued walking towards the car to upload his luggage.

'Why did you lie to me?' I asked aggravated as I followed him towards his car.

'Pass me that suitcase,' he ignored my question and turned to his driver, they began to upload his luggage in the car.

'I'm asking you something,' I stood by his way.

Vikram helped his driver in uploading the suitcase while he ignored me.

'Why did you lie to me?' I repeated irrespective of his behaviour.

'Where did I keep my black bag?' he spoke to the driver instead of answering me.

I yanked his hand furiously and pulled him closer to me. We were mere an inch away, 'I'm asking you something so important and all you are bothered about is your black bag?'

'This is a no parking zone, car can't halt here for more than a minute. Do you understand rules?' Vikram looked deep into my eyes and responded.

'To hell with YOUR rules,' I said.

He turned towards me and looked deep into my eyes.

'Why did you lie to me?' I repeated my question.

'What did I lie to you?' he countered.

'That you and Deepika are seeing each other,' I said.

'I never told you that I'm seeing Deepika, did I?' he shrugged, 'you assumed that I'm seeing her.' Not a single trace of smile on his face.

'Why did you lie about your identity,' I inquired.

'I never lied about my identity. My name is Vikram Khanna, I just didn't tell you that I'm Anuvind Khanna's nephew,' he answered with honesty and modesty.

'And why did you lie that you need the job and you need the promotion,' I asked.

'Of course I needed the job, I didn't lie,' he answered looking into my eyes.

'You are lying, you didn't need the job,' I continued adamantly.

'I needed the job,' he tried to explain.

'Stop lying.' I said. My voice raised. People around us were peering at us by now.

'I'm not lying damn it, I needed the job for myself so that I could see you everyday, I could meet you every day, I could talk to you every day, I never lied to you Shona, not a single word,' his voice raised, he banged his fist and hit on the pole furiously.

He was hurt. I held his hand instantly in mine and tried to soothe him. His hand was swollen red.

'Why did you quit then?' I asked. Tears rolled down my cheeks.

'Because,' his voice was mutated to be relaxed the moment I held his hand in mine. He looked deep into my eyes.

'Tell me,' I asked.

'I couldn't see you with Subrato,' he came closer to me and answered with honesty.

'I am such a fool.' I cried even more.

'I know you are. Say something new,' he half smiled. He wiped my tears. 'Do you know that your nose turns red when you cry.' he mentioned and hugged me to console me. He rubbed my arms. 'Don't cry, you are smudging off your kohl,' he made an attempt to make me smile but all in vain.

He fetched a bottle from his rucksack and offered me some water. My eyes were swollen red. I gulped in some aqua and relaxed myself.

'I want to borrow something from you,' I asked Vikram.

'What?' he countered.

'Your surname,' I said as I kneel down.

'Wait. A girl never proposes,' he said, 'according to #LOVET-ONICS a girl never proposes.....' he continued but I didn't bother to listen.

'A few girls who have the guts, do propose,' I said 'Vikram Khanna I want to borrow your surname will you lend it to me?'

'It is a Punjabi surname not a Bengali one. Do you still want it?' He asked

'I want it,' I answered confidently. 'Mr. Vikram Khanna, WILL YOU MARRY ME,' I asked him still kneeling onto my knees and waiting for his response.

People around us were waiting along with me, a guy in a red turban turned around and his voice cut the crowd to reach us, 'Say a yes dude, she is on her kneels, girls don't do this usually.'

Vikram looked up at me and smiled inevitably *Yes my princess,* he held me up and kissed me along the way.

●●●●●

Praise For Author

SONAM KESWANI - A Daughter, A Sister, A Friend, A Wife, A Mother.....
She has lived each role in her life by giving it more than it deserves....
Inspite of ups and downs in life she never gave up and always stood for her self respect and her Dream.....
A Dream to write until she breathes.....
Its time to live the role of AN AUTHOR who intends to write for herself in pursue of living her Dream.....

Made in United States
Orlando, FL
04 September 2024

51121986R00126